THE MASQUERADES
OF SPRING

THE MASQUERADES OF SPRING

BEN AARONOVITCH

ORION

First published in Great Britain in 2024 by Orion Fiction,
an imprint of The Orion Publishing Group Ltd.,
Carmelite House, 50 Victoria Embankment
London EC4Y 0DZ

An Hachette UK Company

1 3 5 7 9 10 8 6 4 2

A CIP catalogue record for this book is
available from the British Library.

ISBN (Hardback) 978 1 4732 2440 7
ISBN (eBook) 978 1 4732 2442 1

Typeset by Input Data Services Ltd, Bridgwater, Somerset

Printed and bound in Great Britain by Clays Ltd, Elcograf S.p.A.

www.orionbooks.co.uk

For Andrew Cartmel,
who came up with the name in the first place.

I'm crazy about this city.

Toni Morrison, *Jazz*

As I have often opined, what good does it do a fellow to be a master of the mystic arts if he's not allowed to do a bally thing with said mastery? And while I'll admit that knocking the toppers off one's fellow practitioners at Goodwood might have been a tad childish, it hardly, to my mind, constituted a hanging offence. Alas, the old sticks at the Folly didn't see eye to eye with me on this, so I decided that perhaps it would be wise to remove myself somewhere out of their censorious gaze until the blissful waters of Lethe bathed their cares away. Or something.

Since I'm not at all partial to the joys of the rustic, I took a fast liner to New York where the Folly, so I thought, never ventures. (Wrongly, as it happens, but we shall get to that later.)

I found a very pleasant flat – or apartment, as they call it over there – overlooking Washington Square and engaged a valet to handle all the day-to-day necessaries.

In fact, a word about my valet Beauregard is probably in order at this point of the story, before all the *Sturm und Drang* and other Furies have a chance to intrude.

I had arrived at my new apartment in Washington Square and was standing trunkless in an empty hallway when the doorbell rang. Hoping that it might be my luggage, I threw the door open to reveal a tall coloured gentlemen with a long, serious face and a sympathetic manner. When he spoke, it was with one of those cultured southern American accents that rolls around you in a soothing fashion. And I was in need of soothing, being adrift in a foreign city without furniture, or even my baggage.

'My name is Maximillian Beauregard,' he said. 'I believe sir is in need of a valet.'

'Gosh,' I said, and because I had to even yet make inquiries, 'How on earth did you know?'

'You mentioned your need to the elevator operator, sir, and knowing I was looking for a position, he contacted me immediately.'

'I say, that's dashed efficient.'

'Thank you for noticing, sir.'

'You'd better come in,' I said, and the man floated in as if on a cushion of air.

'You wouldn't happen to know where my trunks have got to?' I asked.

'In fact, I encountered them downstairs in the foyer, sir, and took the liberty of engaging some porters to bring them up.'

'Jolly good,' I said. 'And furniture?'

'I'm sure Macy's would be delighted to send over a man with a catalogue, sir.'

'Food?'

'This is New York, sir,' said Beauregard, with just a

touch of *hauteur*. 'Food will not be a problem.'

'You're engaged,' I said.

'Very good, sir.'

An English gentleman of means can live very pleasantly in New York if he's sensible and doesn't upset the natives. Even the local constabulary, who appear to be Fenians to a man, are, with the exception of the odious Sergeant Bracknel, perfectly respectful if you're polite and don't get in their way. There are some very passable restaurants, art galleries and concert halls if high culture is *persona grata*, as it were. But where New York has it over London in spades is modern music, and for the best of that one must venture above 110th Street to the neighbourhood they call Harlem.

There a gentleman can seek out the company of like-minded gentlemen while listening to the best jazz in the world.

So, as you can imagine, as I lay in bed one bright May morning sipping my first reviving cup of coffee, proper tea being beyond my man Beauregard's otherwise extensive capabilities, I was taken aback when the man himself knocked on my door and announced that I had a visitor.

'He's an English gentleman, sir,' said he.

Now all my acquaintances, both English and American, know better than to bother old Augustus before the noon bell, so I did rather wonder who this might be. An unaccountable ripple of apprehension passed over the normally placid surface of my morning routine, but I manfully rose above such turbulence. English visitors are not unheard of, and the steamers did have a habit of docking at an ungodly hour, and so the poor blighter, a stranger in a strange land, might be in need of succour.

And let it never be said of Augustus Berrycloth-Young that he did not rise to the occasion when it came time to cross the street and offer help. Once I was suitably bathed and fortified, that is.

Had I known the truth of it, I would have immediately hidden under my bed and instructed Beauregard to inform my visitor that I had been struck down by the plague during the night.

Instead, I took another sip of the blessed dark fruit of the bean.

'Does this gentleman have a name?' I asked.

'A Mr. Thomas Nightingale,' said Beauregard.

Now, readers of what I suppose I might call my oeuvre might already be familiar with magic, the *demi-monde* and the Folly, but for those of you who have unaccountably hitherto avoided the outpourings of my pen, I shall briefly explain.

Back in the age of enormous wigs, Sir Isaac Newton took time off between inventing gravity and hanging counterfeiters to discover magic. He entrusted this knowledge to a fine upstanding body of gentlemen who formed the Society of the Wise, known to all those in the know as . . . the Folly. From the famous poem, because our illustrious forebears liked a joke as much as the next man. As was the vogue in those days, they founded a school to pass their wisdom on to the next generation, and it was to this prestigious institution that young Augustus was entrusted in the summer of 1914.

It's become fashionable to bemoan one's schooldays, to dwell upon the canings, the cold and the loneliness, but I must say I had a jolly time at school, made some very good chums and, most importantly of all, learnt magic.

You may be thinking, 'Magic, Gussie? My dear boy, there's no such thing!' And that would be because as a respectable graduate of Casterbrook and a member in good standing with the Folly, I am duty-bound to keep the existence of magic hush-hush, *sub rosa*, and on, as they might say here in New York, the down low.

Magic in the wrong hands, or even in no hands at all, can be a dangerous thing, and it was the Folly who was charged with keeping the peace, maintaining order and ensuring the nation's horses went unaffrighted.

This solemn task had made the old sticks at the Folly a grim and humourless bunch who tended to look askance whenever a young wizard, in a moment of exuberance, applied his mighty art to the task of de-helmeting the local constabulary, crockering troublesome strangers or acquiring refreshments at Cheltenham by levitating bottles of champagne away from their coolers. As I mentioned at the beginning, it was to avoid their opprobrium for such a similar trifling matter that I crossed the Atlantic in the first place.

Therefore you can imagine my trepidation upon being informed that the Folly's chief bruno, the man they send forth into the world to solve problems and shoot trouble, one Thomas Nightingale Esquire, was even now loitering at my door.

Still, we graduates of Casterbrook are bywords for fortitude, and rather than fleeing down the fire escape

I instead bade Beauregard to show the Nightingale, for that is how he was often styled, into the living room and offer refreshments while I quickly bathed and dressed.

Beauregard, ever an optimist with regards to the weather, had laid out one of my recently acquired linen suits in dove grey and cut in the 'jazz style', which close acquaintances agreed suited my figure very well. Then, suitably togged up, I stuck my courage to the sticking post and advanced with as much insouciance as I could manage upon the living room.

'What ho, Thomas!' I cried as I entered.

Now, I have often said that the principal difference between the musical offerings of Sissle and Blake, Gershwin and Gershwin, Rodgers and Hart, and those of the likes of Verdi, Tosca and some other bally Italian I have forgotten the name of, is that one might take one's seat for the former with no fear that one will leave the theatre none the wiser with regards to the story. Whereas on those occasions when I have been dragged bodily to the opera, I have spent the entire show trying to work out why Man A is singing angrily at Man B while Woman C trills sadly in the corner. And to rub salt into the wound, as it were, I have the strongest feeling that everybody else in the theatre but me knows exactly what is going on. My friend Lucy, who is an aficionado, tells me that if only I were to read the libretto beforehand then I might stop worrying about the plot and concentrate on the music, which is the main concern of the piece.

It is in this spirit that I feel I should introduce Thomas Nightingale before we, figuratively, meet him on that fateful spring morning so that you, the reader, may have a better understanding of the plot, and in consequence have a heightened appreciation of the music. Otherwise the story might stray into those overlong digressions that are the bane of the modern novel.

He was a tall cove with a chiselled jaw, grey eyes and brown hair that, while cut short at the sides, had a tendency towards unruly behaviour up top. That, and a smooth chin, meant that while he was a good four years older than I, he could, when the mood took him, look younger. He could appear as languid and as carefree as the next young blade. But I had it on good authority that he had dealt with some pretty dicey situations both at home and abroad. Looking at him taking his ease at my window seat and perusing my copy of the *New York Herald Tribune*, I knew trouble. Even when it was wearing a rather fine tweed travelling suit.

'Gussie,' he cried, leaping to his feet and seizing my hand. 'Good to see you. I wonder, if it's not too much trouble, if I may impose upon your hospitality for a couple of nights.'

'Of course,' I cried, while thinking of the many splendid hotels, especially along Broadway, that would be even more ecstatic to receive him as a guest. 'What brings you to New York? Business or pleasure?'

'Business, of course,' he said, and my heart sank, because whereas many members of the Society of the Wise had professional or business interests outside the Folly, Thomas Nightingale was not one of them. If he were in New York on business, it could only be of a magical nature.

'Jolly good,' I said, for want of anything more sensible. I glanced at the clock and saw, with an inward shudder, that it was but a quarter past the hour of ten. Not only an uncivilised hour to be up and awake, but also far too early for lunch. 'Can I offer you some elevenses?'

'Thank you,' he said, 'but your man here has already provided me with coffee.' He glanced at Beauregard, who was floating attentively nearby. 'However, I do need to talk to you in confidence.'

I can take a hint, so after Beauregard had provided me with another blessed and much-needed cup of the bean, I dispatched him off to undertake various errands with the strong intimation that he need not return until after lunch.

Nightingale watched him go and turned to me.

'Sound fellow?' he asked.

'I've always found him so,' I said. 'So what is this dashed business that brings you here? I can assure you I have been as circumspect as a vicar at a christening.'

Nightingale smiled and raised his hand in a most bishop-like beneficence.

'I'm here on quite another matter,' he said. 'One that, given your familiarity with the terrain, I expect you can assist me with.'

'Oh yes?' I said, somewhat guardedly.

'I wish to locate the point of manufacture of a saxophone,' he said.

'A saxophone?' I cried – boggled.

'An enchanted saxophone.'

'What on earth would anyone enchant a saxophone to do?'

8

'In the first instance,' said Nightingale, 'it can impart a greater level of skill to the player. In the second instance, when played correctly, this one can talk.'

I was agog.

'What does it say?' I asked.

'That depends on the musician,' said Nightingale. 'The chap who owned it had learnt how to play "hallo", "yes" and "no". But as far as the boffins could determine, the instrument had no will of its own. It said, or rather sang, what its owner played.'

The owner, in this case, was one Laurence Ellwood, a Jamaican chap who had arrived in London by way of New York.

'Have you ever heard of him?' asked Nightingale.

'Can't say I have,' I said, although I knew Lucy would know. Lucy had a mind like one of those bally card catalogues they have in libraries. If you have ever puckered, plucked, bowed or sung in New York, then Lucy will have your details. It can be uncanny, and would have been dashed useful had I any intention of introducing Lucy to the Nightingale, or vice versa. But I have learnt from bitter experience to keep certain parts of my world separate from the others.

'No matter,' said Nightingale. 'Mr. Ellwood was quite co-operative when it became clear that we were willing to replace the instrument with one of an equal but unenchanted quality. Plus a finder's fee, of course.'

'Of course,' I said.

Mr. Ellwood did furnish Nightingale with the name and address of the pawn shop from whence he had acquired the instrument. I'd never been there myself, but one of the benefits of the American obsession of laying out their towns in grids is that addresses are easy to find.

This one was on West 47th Street, close to the corner with Tenth Avenue, deep inside the neighbourhood known as Hell's Kitchen. A well-deserved name for an area with a terrible reputation for criminality and danger. Lucy had cautioned me against setting foot in the place, so of course Nightingale was all for heading out there on the instant.

Well, it seemed like a rum thing, but we wizards have a code and never let it be said that Augustus Berrycloth-Young shirked his duty as a keeper of the secret flame. Not that I have the faintest idea where the secret flame might possibly be, although I assume that's because it is a secret.

In any case, I rose to the occasion and we hailed a rather fetching green and red taxicab and set forth for 47th Street.

The shop itself was a sort of cluttered Aladdin's cave with two glass counters. There was a cornucopia of watches, rings and silver cutlery under glass in the counters, and ranks of musical instruments, barometers and rifles along the walls. A line of trumpets hung from hooks like skinned rabbits next to what I am sure was a bally balalaika, or possibly a lute.

Stacked in the gaps were teetering piles of steamer trunks and suitcases showing, I presumed, a great deal of confidence amongst newly arrived travellers that New York was their final destination. A sign above a back counter proclaimed LOAN DEPARTMENT and DIAMONDS APPRAISED.

I was assailed by a hundred types of *vestigium* – have I explained *vestigia* yet? No? For trained practitioners, it's easy to forget that most people don't recognise a *vestigium* when they encounter it. Quite simply, magic, even the magic of the everyday, leaves behind a trace which old Isaac called a *vestigium*. You probably encounter it every day, but dismiss it as a random sound or smell or a passing fancy. It is as insubstantial as a daydream and most often, even to the magically trained, as useful.

In any case, locations such as pawn shops, libraries and lost property stores accumulate a great many of these whispers and fancies, and so I ignored them now as irrelevant.

But Augustus, the reader might cry, if this *vestig—* whatnot is irrelevant, what was the point of that whole paragraph? To which I can only counsel patience, dear reader; *vestigia* will become relevant soon enough.

A stout man with a square face, a savage moustache and an inappropriately snazzy homburg hat graced us with a nod and a minatory gaze.

'How may I help you, gentlemen?' he said in a manner that suggested that in truth he would rather not provide any such help.

'A friend of mine purchased a musical instrument from this shop last year,' said Nightingale.

'No refunds,' said the homburg.

'A refund will not be necessary,' said Nightingale. 'We're merely looking for some information.'

'Are you cops?'

'No,' said Nightingale.

'You a Seamus?' The man pronounced 'you' as if it had a *z* at the end.

Nightingale glanced at me and raised an inquiring eyebrow.

'Private detective,' I said.

'No,' said Nightingale, turning back to the man with the ferocious moustache. 'A friend of ours bought a musical instrument here and we'd merely like to establish who originally pledged it.'

Nightingale showed the man the receipt, but the man looked unimpressed or, just possibly, uncomprehending.

Nightingale was about to repeat his explanation when the man shook his head.

'Sorry, mac,' he said. 'Can't help you.'

'I'm willing to make it worth your while,' said Nightingale.

This caught the man's immediate attention, and he indicated that he was desirous to see the colour of our money. It was at this point that Nightingale revealed that he was indeed fatally short of American currency, and asked me to step in and shoulder the financial burden. I would be lying if I said I wasn't a little put out at having my ear bitten in so cavalier a fashion. But I could hardly say this in front of the moustache, and so I rustled up the rhino. And if Nightingale proved a little over-generous in his estimation of how much this moustache's time was worth, then I did not feel that just then was the appropriate moment to mention it.

Things took a turn for the rummy when the moustache asked to examine the receipt again, but when Nightingale unwisely handed the thing over, he stuffed it into the maw that, rather alarmingly, opened under his bristling lip hedge. Then he chewed thoughtfully for a moment or two before swallowing.

They say that ignorance is bliss, and in fact that is the unofficial motto of the Folly, but had our moustachioed friend had any inkling of who he was dealing with, what followed might not have come as such a surprise.

He certainly wouldn't have given Nightingale that challenging 'And what are you going to do about it?' look. Not if he, like me, had ever watched Nightingale play indoor tennis.

'I see,' said Nightingale. 'I thought it was a very fair bribe. Wouldn't you say so, Gussie?'

'Generous,' I said and, because I was still stung by the expense, 'More than generous, in fact.'

'I'm going to count to five,' said Nightingale, 'and before I reach the end you will provide us with the information we seek, or,' he glanced over his shoulder to flash a grin at me, 'return my friend's investment.'

Moustache bristled, neither option being to his taste.

Even as Nightingale reached the number two, he opened that fearsome sub-mustachio maw and bellowed, 'Jake! Get your ass out here!'

Then the poor deluded fool gave Nightingale the sort of smug look your rival gives you when you slice your ball into a bunker on the first hole, thinking the match is all over bar the counting out of winnings. In response, Nightingale stopped counting and waited for Jake.

Jake, another stout man in a homburg, but this time mercifully clean-shaven, arrived a full ten seconds later, bursting through a door at the back and brandishing a shotgun. Before he could take aim, Nightingale, without taking his eyes off the moustache, made a small gesture with his left hand. As if by invisible hands, the shotgun was wrenched from Jake's grasp and sent skidding across the floor to stop at my feet. Simultaneously, the poor man was pitched forward and slammed into the ground. There was a crack and a pained grunt.

'Gussie,' said Nightingale. 'Keep an eye on him for me, old boy.'

I would be lying if I said I didn't relish the chance to have a bit of a magical tussle, although it did seem a bit unsporting to inflict spells upon unsuspecting shopkeepers. I'm all for snatching off a policeman's helmet or pulling a prank upstairs at the Folly or the Bliss, but this seemed a mite more serious. That worried me.

The moustache reached under the counter, no doubt seeking a weapon of his own, but froze when something bright and metallic flashed past his face. One of a myriad drawers behind him had opened and a dozen or so table knives had floated out to orbit his head.

Judging correctly that any sudden moves would be unwise, the man straightened slowly until he was staring at Nightingale with his eyes bulging in surprise. They flicked back and forth, vainly trying to track the knives as they flashed past his face.

'Now,' said Nightingale, 'let us start our conversation again.'

'Just who is "the Killer"?' asked Nightingale as we left the pawn shop.

'A Mr. Madden,' I said. 'Top gangster of this parish. Those two were probably in his employ, or even more likely, under his protection.'

'Aha,' said Nightingale, with a delighted and wholly inappropriate grin. 'This must be one of those famous "protection rackets" I've read about.'

'The very same,' I said gloomily.

'So when he warned us that this "Killer" would be taking an interest, that was in the nature of a threat?' said Nightingale.

I indicated that indeed that was the case, although this did not seem to concern Nightingale one jot. An attitude that roused me to a state of ire at odds with my normally sunny disposition.

'I say, Thomas, you may be planning to hop off back to Blighty on the next liner, but I happen to like it here,' I said. 'And I'd rather you didn't queer the pitch.'

'Gussie?' said Nightingale with some surprise. 'Are you planning to settle?'

'What if I am?' I said.

'Good for you,' he said. 'I wouldn't worry about "the Killer". I've dealt with these types of ruffians before. They're all bluster and they're as terrified of . . . Mr. Madden, was it?'

'Owney Madden,' I said.

'Welsh?' asked Nightingale.

'Born in Leeds, apparently.'

'Those men will be as terrified of Mr. Owney Madden as anyone else,' he said. 'And since nothing was lost from the shop except their pride, they're unlikely to bring it to his attention. These gangsters have little time for subordinates who waste their time.'

While it sounded dashed plausible, I decided that I would endeavour to avoid Hell's Kitchen in future. If only to put Lucy's mind at rest.

Since finding an available cab in Hell's Kitchen was unlikely, we had started strolling east towards the theatre district. It must have rained while we were in the jumble-sale cave of wonders, for the streets were washed clean and gleaming in the spring sunshine. New York is at its best on days such as these, when it's fresh and full of possibilities. On such days it's hard to feel anything less than the jolly old *joie de vivre*. And the savage moustachioed one had, with some reluctance, given us a name.

'A name is not much to go on,' said Nightingale.

'*Au contraire*,' I said with, I think, a justifiable degree of smugness. 'We know that he played the saxophone. That should be enough.'

'Are you certain?'

'I know a man,' I said. 'In Harlem.'

Before we transport our scene to Harlem, I feel I should explain about Lucy. Before I can do that, I must make a confession which may come as a shock to many of my readers since it is an aspect of my life that I have kept hitherto under a veil. Before reading further, many of you may wish to ensure that you are comfortably seated with a restorative tipple ready within easy reach.

As well as a practitioner of magic, I am, in fact, also a practitioner of what they call 'the love that dare not speak its name'. Back in old Blighty, a chap like me, of reasonable means and eccentric reputation, can live a carefree life providing, of course, he doesn't make the grievous error of speaking that name out loud. In London a chap merely needs to know which clubs one might frequent or whose soirées to gather at, and when uncertain, a phrase or two in Polari will settle any doubts.

The trouble with moving to New York was that I was ignorant of the appropriate venues, and cheerfully greeting someone as *duckie* and asking whether they are having a *bona day* garners only a puzzled frown. And of course the problem with the love that dare not speak its name is that you dare not speak its name. A bit of a conundrum, you might say. Until one night, while I was shaking a leg at Connie's and I chanced to catch Lucy's eye. Or, more precisely, he caught mine.

Poets and romantic authors alike speak of love at first sight, but up until that fateful night I had been sceptical. My liaisons had been short and sweet and uncomplicated and, I like to think, mutually satisfactory. But I had never before been, as it were, so mortally struck by Cupid's arrow.

There he was, leaning casually against the wall on the edge of the dance floor, his eyes flicking between the band on stage and a reporter's notebook in which he made occasional marks with a silver propelling pencil.

He was a coloured man, taller than me, with a fine, well-shaped head and a full, sensuous mouth. He wore that night – and, to my despair, on every subsequent occasion – a finely tailored but rumpled tweed suit. His eyes, half-hidden behind round gold-rimmed spectacles, were a startlingly intelligent brown. I did not realise I had stopped moving until one of the other dancers stumbled in to me. I apologised without looking round and, as if drawn by an invisible lasso, drifted towards this personification of Adonis in tweed.

I floated to a stop before him, he looked down, and our eyes met.

'Excuse me,' he said. 'You're blocking my view of the band.'

I moved out of his way and he gave me an apologetic smile before turning his full attention to the stage. Now, the practice of magic takes both concentration and patience, and it was the latter quality that allowed me to stand next to this personification of Eros for a whole two minutes, watching him take meticulous notes in shorthand, before I could stand it no longer and was forced to speak.

'I say,' I said. 'Are you a reporter, what?'

'What makes you think that?' he asked, never taking his eyes from his notebook.

'I thought the bally notebook was bit of a giveaway,' I said, feeling like a man floundering in the sea. 'Unless you're stealing the songs.' My head going under for the second time. 'But I wouldn't recommend it.' That was it. I was lost, drowned in a sea of inarticulacy and coming to a sad end. Just as my old headmaster predicted I would.

Lucy turned and looked at me over the gold rims of his spectacles.

'Why wouldn't you?' he asked.

I'd say I was drowning in his eyes, but then I would be drowning twice and Lucy, who often amuses himself by reading these missives prior to publication, would complain that I am complicating my metaphors beyond the point of comprehension. Having read some of the modern stuff turned out these days by the Bloomsbury set, I'm rather more inclined to think I was ahead of my time.

Still, metaphors aside, I managed to assemble a sentence that would pass muster.

'I don't think they're particularly good,' I said, and then, because Lucy's eyes never left mine, 'Not a patch on Bix Beiderbecke. Wouldn't you agree?'

There was a long pause while he considered this and I went down for the third and final time. Then he smiled and it was like the sun rising over an oasis in the desert. Which, thankfully, meant I was no longer drowning, but at the same time equally lost.

'Have you heard Gladys Bentley yet?' he asked.

I said I had not, which only made the smile wider.

'I think it's time we blow this scene,' he said, and

half an hour later we were downstairs at a speakeasy on 133rd Street, breathing smoke, drinking terrible hooch and listening to a young coloured girl in a bow tie and short Eton jacket sing and play the piano all the way to morning.

Later, when I told Lucy about the love that dare not speak its name, he held me close and said that it may not speak its name, 'But it sure as shit sings the blues.'

Lucy – or, more formally, Lucien Gibbs – worked in what he liked to call the Negro end of Madison Avenue. There he earned a living writing copy for advertisements to be placed in newspapers and magazines. He pretended to me that he had no interest in the work, but I noticed that he was quick enough to draw my attention to this work when he encountered it in, as it were, the wild. His first love, of course, was his study and writing about the work, lives and scandals of New York's musicians and singers. As I believe I've intimated before, Lucy's knowledge of such was without peer, and it was in his capacity as an enormous brain that I now planned to consult him.

I left Nightingale loitering outside the office and went in.

'What ho, Gussie,' called Loretta, the company secretary. She greets me thus every time I come into the office and, for some unfathomable reason, finds it a source of tremendous good fun.

'What ho, Lotty,' I halloed back, which only provoked further giggling. 'Is the brain about?'

Still laughing, Loretta pointed upwards.

*

I skipped past the offices of what Lucy was pleased to call his 'fellow toilers in the pit of lies'. Then I trotted up half a dozen flights of stairs until I emerged onto the roof. There I found Lucy working at the mechanical monster that he laughably referred to as his 'portable'. The beast, which must have weighed a stone or more, sat upon a rickety card table, and the action was so stiff that Lucy was forced to use a heavy hand when typing. Between the smashing of the keys, the groaning of the table and Lucy's own mumbled soliloquy, he rarely noticed my approach. I didn't like to disturb him when he was in full flow, so I waited. There was a rhythm to his work, so I knew there'd be a pause ere long.

Summer in New York can get infernally hot. And during that season, the whole population migrates to the roofs of their apartments and, in the absence of proper balconies, their fire escapes. Sensible people, my expatriate friends assure me, depart for Cape Cod and other points upstate.

As a result, the roof of your average New York block of flats can sport a wondrous collection of garden furniture, flower beds, pigeon lofts and, astonishingly, beehives. Lucy's rooftop hideaway boasted a large marquee tent of the kind you see sheltering the masses at village fêtes on wet Sunday afternoons in the country. This allowed Lucy to labour on the roof even in the most inclement weather. Rain or snow, Lucy said that he worked best when he could look up and see Harlem spread out before him. That day, he sat in the warm afternoon sun, his well-shaped head bent over his work. There was a sudden pause in both the typing and the soliloquy, but I hesitated, having been wrong-footed before.

'At the *better* fountains everywhere,' he cried in triumph, before banging the sentence into being. Then he turned to regard me over the rim of his spectacles.

'Gussie,' he said. 'What on earth are you doing here?'

I took a quick look over the parapet to make sure Nightingale hadn't happened to anyone, but he seemed quite content to lean on his cane and watch the passers-by.

'I have a favour to ask,' I said, and filled him in on the quest to discover the source of the magical speaking saxophone. Although, of course, I left out both the magical and the speaking parts. Lucy joined me at the parapet and gazed down at Nightingale.

'Is that him?' he asked.

Whenever he stands that close to me, I have a deuced time restraining myself from touching him. But even alone on a roof, it was best to play it safe.

'What was the musician's name?' he asked.

'David Edwards.'

'Saxophone, you say?'

Lucy's face took on the aspect of Aristotle thinking upon Achilles and the tortoise, and he snapped his fingers a dozen times. A sure-fire sign that the magnificent brain was bent to the task.

The snapping stopped and he looked at me.

'You're sure he was a saxophonist?'

'We know he once owned one,' I said, because the masters at my old school had made it very clear that even one as dense as I needed to be precise. Magic can be dangerous if you don't pay attention to the details.

'Purlie Edwards,' said Lucy. 'Used to play the trumpet before the war. I did hear he switched sometime after, but he quit this years ago. He's the Reverend Edwards now. Over at the Church of Jesus Christ the Holy on Seventh and 140th.'

I thanked Lucy and went to leave, but nothing would do but that he would accompany me and Nightingale to the church to facilitate the encounter.

'And besides, I want to meet this Nightingale,' he said. 'And you've piqued my curiosity about this matter. I want to know what's really going on.'

'What makes you think something is going on?'

'You've always claimed to be a man of independent means,' he said.

'I am,' I said. 'Very independent.'

'And yet you say this Nightingale's name as if you worked for him,' said Lucy, and then cocked his head to one side. 'No, that's not right. You say it as if he's your superior officer. That's odd, even allowing for the fact that you're both English. Are you secretly in the army, Gussie?'

I don't need to explain to you how absurd is the notion that Augustus Berrycloth-Young would don the uniform under any circumstances short of an invasion by Martians. And that very absurdity helped me come up with a plausible explanation.

'We went to school together,' I said. 'It's an English thing.'

*

'*Thomas,*' I said. 'This is my good friend Lucien Gibbs. Lucien, this is Thomas Nightingale, who is an old chum from school.'

Lucy and Thomas shook hands. Both, to my mind, eyeing each other with equal amounts of suspicion. I was reminded, after my months in New York, away from the Folly, just why one does not mix one's social circles. Especially when both walk in the shadows, albeit different shadows. Possibly on two completely different streets.

'So what was the name of the school?' asked Lucy.

'It was a very minor school,' said Nightingale. 'You wouldn't have heard of it.'

'Shall I hail us a cab?' I asked quickly.

'It's not far,' said Lucy. 'If you two fine gentlemen are up for a stroll.'

I used to think that my old school took sport seriously. Nightingale earned much of his reputation playing rugger, cricket and indoor tennis, and so was a darling of the masters. But over here they take it very seriously indeed, as evinced by the fact that they call a chap who takes more than a passing interest in a particular sport 'a fan'. Short for fanatic, don't you see? Even so, it was something of a surprise to walk into a church and find a basketball game in progress. Refereed by, Lucy pointed out, the Reverend Edwards himself.

In fact, the venue looked more like a gymnasium than a place of worship, although I could see where the pews were stacked neatly against the walls. The players were all schoolboys, who ran up and down the court yelling excitedly. I looked at Nightingale and caught a wistful expression on his face. We were content to watch the game until its finish, especially Lucy, who is a 'fan' of the sport.

'We should have played this at Casterbrook,' said Nightingale, no doubt imagining himself as captain of yet another school team.

After the Reverend Edwards had blown his whistle and waved the boys off to change and go home, he stopped and gave us a long stare. He was one of those short blighters who come across as much bigger than they really are, with a fairer complexion than Lucy and his hair marcelled into obedience.

'Purlie?' said Lucy, and the Reverend's stare lost much of its hostility, at least as far as Lucy was concerned. When he turned his gaze on Nightingale and me it reacquired a distinctly frosty aspect.

'Mr. Gibbs,' said Edwards. 'What brings you to the House of the Lord?'

'I'm guiding these two gentlemen toward the Promised Land,' said Lucy.

'I see,' said Edwards, his lips twitching and some of the frost evaporating. 'It's not enough that they come up for the music and the dancing, but they want some of that Negro spirituality as well.'

'Information, Mr. Edwards,' said Nightingale. 'That's what we want.'

Edwards was suddenly wary.

'Are you with the police, sir?' he said with a deference that belied his former hostility.

'No, they're not,' said Lucy with a sharp note I

recognised as anger, although blow me if I knew what he was angry about.

'We're collectors,' I said. 'From London.'

'Well, unless you're coming to collect my pews,' said Edwards, indicating where a number of parishioners were heaving the aforementioned off their stacks and laying them out, 'I doubt I have anything you gentlemen will want. Although salvation is available for everyone – even the English.'

'That's a relief,' I said.

'We're interested in the provenance of the saxophone you pawned five years ago,' said Nightingale.

'I always knew that instrument would come back to haunt me,' he said. 'You know it's cursed, right?'

'Hence our interest,' said Nightingale.

'You're interested in things that have been touched by the Devil?'

'Our principals are,' said Nightingale. 'They like to be sure that such things are kept safely away where they won't do any harm.'

'I never redeemed it,' said Edwards. 'It's either still at the store or they sold it.'

'The item itself has come into our possession,' said Nightingale. 'What interests us is where it came from.'

'You don't want to get involved in that business,' said Edwards. 'Trust me.'

'What business is that?'

'The music business, Mr. Nightingale,' said Edwards, looking narrow-eyed at Nightingale. 'It's the Devil's business and no mistake.'

'Is that why you gave it up?' asked Lucy suddenly. 'You've never said.'

'You never asked me before, Lucien,' said Edwards, turning to Lucien and, it seemed to me, quite pleased to change the conversation. 'That was down to the war. You probably don't know the details.' He turned back to Nightingale and me. 'But these two fine European gentlemen might. If I speak of the Ardennes in the fall of 1918, is that enlightening? I was a Rattler in the 396th, a coloured regiment so fearsome that our own army was scared of us and made us fight beside the French.'

'Ah,' said Nightingale in recognition, but I didn't have the slightest notion of what, so I nodded along thoughtfully. It's a technique, by the way, I recommend to any of you who have friends steeped in serious purpose or otherwise intellectually inclined. I've always believed that it's better to stay quiet and encourage such people to believe you're hanging on their every word, rather than foolishly open your mouth and give evidence to the contrary. In truth, committing the strings of *formae*, from which spells are derived, to memory while at school proved excellent training.

'They call us the Hellfighters now, the Harlem Hellfighters,' said Edwards. 'But that was the name of the band, and what a band they were. Williams, Taylor, Hawkins, Storms. I was good but I never made the cut. Company bugler, that was me. Reveille to get them up and Taps to put them to bed.'

Edwards fell silent then and looked down at his shoes. He stayed like that for so long that his parishioners finished laying out the pews and lined up in a respectful silence to wait for him.

'I thought music was my life, but after the war there was too much death mixed in with it,' he said finally. 'I switched to the sax because I had some notion that would make a difference, but no. I had to find some way of making the music holy again. You understand that, right? Lucien? You need to understand that. The music will take you down among devils if you ain't careful.' He nodded at me and Nightingale. 'The devils.'

'So where did the saxophone come from?' asked Nightingale.

'It was given to me,' said Edwards. 'By the spawn of Satan himself.'

3

It would probably come as a surprise to the Reverend Peter Warmsly, who led school prayers at Casterbrook, that the Devil's name was Mark Harper. The Rev. himself had always contended that the Devil was in all of us and that it was our responsibility to thwart him at every opportunity. Much of this thwarting involved resisting the temptation to handle one's private parts – a prohibition many of us circumvented by handling each other's privates instead. Lucy called this, when I told him about it, the law of unintended consequences. Still, judging from the way the equally Reverend Edwards spat out his name, Mark Harper had done much more than a little late-night self-abuse.

'I assume you know this man's whereabouts,' said Nightingale to Lucy once we were back out on the pavement.

'Mr. Harper is a music publisher,' he said. 'Has an office on Tin Pan Alley.'

'And where is this alley located?' asked Nightingale.

If you've been to a show anytime recently, or listened to a modern record, then the chances are that the music publisher – the chap who owns the music and makes the money – has an office on West 28th Street, otherwise known to the *cognoscenti* as Tin Pan Alley for reasons that not even Lucy can explain.

Mark Harper worked from an untidy office on the top floor of a shabby building that proved to be a noisy hive of similarly small offices. As we climbed the stairs, a cacophony of pianos, violins and human voices, raised in song or in anger, assailed us. I couldn't help feeling a sense of desperation permeating the whole place. Nightingale appeared unaffected.

Lucy had declined to accompany us, and instead said he would take the opportunity to run some errands and meet us outside when we were finished. I couldn't for the life of me think of what errands he might have to run, but if my acquaintance with Lucy has taught me one thing, it is that the life of an advertising executive is full of mystery.

Mr. Harper was one of those thin fair-haired men from whom the colour has drained as they get older, until one gets the impression that one is talking to an old photograph that has come to sudden life. His office was ruthlessly tidy but the furniture and carpet were worn. Mr. Harper, to my mind, had obviously seen better days. Perhaps this had made him dyspeptic, because Nightingale and I had barely crossed his threshold before he ordered us to leave in the coarsest of terms.

'F—k off,' he said again as Nightingale advanced into his office with me as his discreet shadow.

'Good afternoon,' said Nightingale. 'Are you Mr. Mark Harper?'

'Are you deaf?' asked Mr. Harper. 'I don't care what you're selling. I'm not buying.'

'I'm not selling, sir,' said Nightingale, and sat in one of the two rickety wooden chairs in front of the desk. I gingerly took my place in the other.

Mr. Harper's mouth opened and his face took on a fine shade of crimson at our effrontery, which was only ameliorated a *soupçon* when Nightingale explained that we were there in pursuit of a purchase. At least the mouth, a large pink maw inhabited by unnaturally white dentures, remained closed as he listened.

'We believe you provided Mr. Edwards with the saxophone in question,' finished Nightingale.

Mr. Harper squinted at us like a fishmonger eyeing a troublesome flounder. He might have been deep in thought, or perhaps having difficulty with his digestion. It was hard to tell which. Then a look of naked loathing crossed his face, aimed not at us, but at some inward memory.

'The Doughman has her,' he said, and then, noting our looks of bafflement, he went on to explain. 'Steven Baker knows all about the saxophone – and other things.'

Nightingale asked where we might find this Mr. Baker, which caused Mr. Harper to turn dyspeptic all over again.

'He runs a joint on Lenox Avenue,' he said in an airy, disparaging tone. 'Name of the Alexandra. That's where you'll find him.'

'He was lying,' said Nightingale as soon as we were out of the building.

'Was he?' I asked. 'I thought he looked rummy. What do you think he was lying about?'

'Ah,' said Nightingale, 'my dear Gussie. Therein lies our difficulty. Let us see where this lead takes us before we circle back to Mr. Harper and run him to ground.'

'Are we looking for magic instruments or hunting foxes?' I asked.

'I see your good friend Mr. Gibbs approaching,' he said. 'He should be able to guide us to the Alexandra.'

We hailed a cab back uptown. Travelling by taxi in the company of Lucy can be dicey, as some cabbies refuse to carry coloured passengers even when accompanied by whites. This time, the driver – a solid brute in a flat cap – seemed unperturbed.

'Tin Pan Alley to Lenox Avenue,' Lucy murmured once we were safely under way. 'He figures I'm a musician and you're my manager.'

'Excellent,' said Nightingale. 'That's a story that has potential to get us through the front door.'

Although, in the event the front doors were propped open by a mop and bucket, so we entered freely.

There can be few things that lack cheeriness quite as much as a nightclub seen during the day. The stage and the dance floor always seem smaller, the gilt and velvet tarnished and grubby. Voices echo amongst the stacked chairs and empty tables. Especially mine.

'I say, hallo! Is anyone home?'

'Stop,' said Nightingale. 'Can you feel that?'

I dutifully stopped and let my eyes close. I could

definitely feel something: a smell of pine and the whisper of the wind amongst leaves, and through it a dainty little tune. Something Continental, played on a fiddle or a flute.

'Feel what?' asked Lucy.

'Certain places accumulate . . .' Nightingale paused, looking for a word. 'A vibration, if you like. A memory of a certain category of event.'

'What kind of an event?'

'Unusual events of a specific type,' said Nightingale, and to me: 'Can you feel it?'

I told him I could.

'That was a less than helpful answer,' said Lucy.

'No doubt Gussie can explain,' said Nightingale. 'But later. Not here, not now.'

Up on the bandstand, a coloured chap was practising a phrase on one of those modern shortened grand pianos in the so-called 'stride' idiom. He looked up as we approached and – to nobody's surprise, save perhaps Nightingale's – recognised Lucy.

They greeted each other in a friendly fashion and we were introduced as fellow jazz aficionados from London. The pianist's name was Lloyd Beaumont, and he joked that he'd come north to New York so he could avoid singing the blues. Pretty soon we were having a friendly disagreement about whether Fats Waller owed anything to James P. Johnson, with Lloyd having the unfair advantage of being able to make his points by playing quotations on the ivories. In fact, we got so chummy that I didn't notice Nightingale had evaporated away until he drifted back.

'Perhaps you can help satisfy my curiosity,' said Nightingale.

Lloyd shrugged and said he would if he could.

'We've heard rumours that the owner of this establishment has access to musical instruments of extraordinary quality,' he said. 'Have you ever heard anything like that?'

Lloyd's left hand danced back and forth to the bass notes on the piano.

'This baby is quite a sweet thing if you know how to treat her,' he said.

'Yes it is,' said Nightingale. 'But I'm thinking of something a little more unusual.'

I saw Lucy wanted to speak, but I put a hand on his arm to quell him.

'Unusual how?' asked Lloyd.

'Imbued with an unusual spirit,' said Nightingale. 'That meant it was played not just better, but much better than you thought the musician warranted.'

'Can't say as I have. Beyond, you know, the usual magic,' said Lloyd, and played a chord.

'Nothing strange at all?' asked Nightingale.

'Ha,' said Lloyd. 'This is Harlem. Just about everything's strange here. Mr. Baker did have this creepy frail that he used to bring around.'

'Creepy?' asked Nightingale. 'How?'

'Very tall and long and pale,' said Lloyd. 'Always wore a veil over her face. Used to drift around the club when there was dancing. Never spoke, never smoked. Like I said, creepy.' Lloyd grinned at me and Lucy. 'Loved the music, though. You could tell. You can always tell the true believers from the dilettantes. During sets you'd find her dancing backstage. Terrible dancer, too, couldn't keep time worth a damn, used to wave her arms around like she was a tree in the wind. I reckoned she was kicking the gong around.'

But, he admitted, he hadn't seen her around for a while.

Nightingale asked after Purlie Edwards, and Lloyd said he remembered him playing a few nights at the Alexandra and some other clubs and bars. He'd played the sax back then; in fact, Lloyd was quite surprised he'd played the trumpet before the war.

'He was definitely cokey back then. A lot of the Hell-fighters went that way after the war,' said Lloyd. 'I heard he cleaned himself up and took up preaching over on 140th.'

As we left, Lloyd called after Lucy.

'I'm expecting a good review in the next edition,' he said.

'Only if you play somewhere they let me in the damn audience,' Lucy called back.

We retired to a little place on 133rd Street and introduced Nightingale to properly cooked fried chicken. I'd recently become very familiar with Harlem cuisine since the restaurants downtown were strangely reluctant to serve Lucy – which was, in his opinion, no great loss. Harlem, Lucy contends, contains all that a man might need. Including, and this part used to puzzle me, the illusion of freedom.

Mr. Steven Baker III had been nowhere to be found.

'I did have a chance to have a quick look through his

office desk,' said Nightingale, who apparently had made good use of his period of evaporation. 'But I didn't find anything useful. Something unusual had spent time in there, if I'm any judge.'

'When you say unusual,' said Lucy, 'what do you mean?'

'How much has Gussie told you about magic?' asked Nightingale.

It is said that the one rule about the Folly is you don't talk about the Folly, and this is true providing you ignore all the other rules, including the prohibition on playing indoor tennis on the upper balcony. But it is fair to say that from our first day at Casterbrook, we were urged to discretion. Magic is fabulously dangerous to the untrained would-be practitioner, and it was better that the general public were kept ignorant of its existence so they wouldn't be tempted to experiment and hurt themselves.

But Gussie, the more observant and better read amongst you cry, if discretion is your watchword, how do you explain your de-toppering activities at Goodwood, or the occasional bout of constabulary de-helmeting, or that time you enchanted a tree in Kew Gardens to sing the 'Flower Duet' from *Lakmé*?

Aha, I answer, you'll notice that none of those japes had any lasting consequences, nor were they so obvious that anybody other than a fellow practitioner would notice. So I must say I was a bit miffed by Nightingale's breezy assumption that I had fessed up everything to Lucy.

'When you say magic is real, what do you mean?' said

Lucy, who, as I have indicated, is as sharp as a tack. 'Are you talking Houdini or hoodoo?'

'The latter,' said Nightingale. 'Although we don't call it that.'

There was a long pause in the conversation which I took advantage of to address my fried chicken, which truly deserved a great deal more attention than it was getting from both Lucy and Nightingale. Fried chicken is one of America's great contributions to world culture. One which has been sorely overlooked by both natives and incomers alike.

'Can anyone know when something is "unusual", or is this a special ability only available to smartly dressed Englishmen?' asked Lucy.

'Think of it as being like able to tell ragtime from stride,' I said. 'Everybody can tell there's a difference, but you have to know music to understand what the difference is.'

'I'm sure Gussie can explain in detail later,' said Nightingale. 'The important thing is that something of a magical nature has spent time in that club.'

'Recently?' asked Lucy.

'That's hard to say,' said Nightingale. 'It would depend on the intensity of the original source. Do you think the owner will be there tonight?'

Lucy said that he thought it likely, and that is when Nightingale developed a sudden desire to sample the night life of New York in general, and the Alexandra in particular. I agreed to take him only on the basis that the sooner we located these enchanted instruments, the sooner Nightingale would return home. Lucy declared that he would return to his office and catch up on his work, but not before making it clear that he and I would be discussing recent developments in more detail later.

Rather than look for a cab on Lenox Avenue, I introduced Nightingale to the delights of the New York subway, which is every bit the equal of the Underground. We arrived back at my flat to find that Beauregard had prepared the guest room and unpacked Nightingale's steamer trunk, which had been delivered while we were out. I pleaded fatigue, retired to my bedroom, and had Beauregard bring me a brandy and soda.

'Go easy with the soda and splash the brandy about with abandon,' I told him.

Prohibition, that bizarre aberration of the American spirit, could be dashed confusing to someone raised in the free and easy metrop of old London. New Yorkers seemed just as keen on their booze as the chaps back home, but every so often some bally politico would declare that they were dead set on enforcing the Velocipede Act, although quite what it had to do with bicycles I never understood, and close down clubs and speakeasies willy-nilly. New Yorkers, to a man, woman and child, regarded these spasms in much the way a Londoner regards rain and fog. Dashed inconvenient, but one of those things that are beyond the ken of mortal man and not something that could be allowed to interfere with the social whirl.

One unfortunate upshot, however, was that the available booze was often appalling. They call much of it 'bathtub gin', and they are not joking about the bathtub. As a result I tried to be parsimonious with my imported brandy, while letting Beauregard siphon off a bottle or two as a side benefit. I would have welcomed Nightingale with far greater *bonhomie* had he brought a case or two of the good stuff with him.

I wanted to be with Lucy, not least so I could reassure him about the magic, but we could never risk him staying the night at the flat, and there was no chance of me slipping away for a tryst at his place while Nightingale was here.

I lay on my bed, nursing my brandy and soda, and closed my eyes until the old bean had stopped spinning. Now, many of those who know me, including no few members of my own family, regard me as something of a dunce, and I will be the first to admit that I have never been what some might call a 'serious' person. Still, you didn't have to be a brain to see that there was more to the current caper than interest in a stray saxophone, no matter how magical it might be. For one thing, I had always been led to believe that the good old United States was off limits to the Folly due to some unpleasantness involving the 1812 Overture, and that visiting practitioners were admonished not to practise while visiting.

And, for another, Thomas Nightingale was, if the rumours were to be believed, the Folly's top man, the one sent out to deal with dastardly foreign plots and intractable disputes. If he were in New York, it was for a damned good reason, and one thing was for certain: the well-being and happiness of Augustus Berrycloth-Young Esquire would not be a priority.

Still, it is also said of good old Berrycloth-Young that

we are surprisingly hardy in the face of adversity, and quick to spring back from whatever unkind blows the cruel hand of fate may land upon us.

The best thing, I surmised, was to help Nightingale finish his business as swiftly as possible, with as little involvement from me as possible, and then wave him off at the docks. That was the ticket, I thought, and, fortified by the last of my brandy and soda, I arose and stepped forth to see what selection Beauregard had made for this evening's entertainment.

Now, there are philistines, and the sort of barbarians that were said to have plagued ancient Rome, who assert that one tuxedo is much like any other. The evening wear laid out for me was a beautiful deep blue, and the trousers, while still straight, had a pleat so that they fell in a much more becoming manner. The jacket was high-waisted but didn't have the raked pockets that set apart my newer suits.

Once we had both dressed, Nightingale and I met in the living room to use the wall mirror and make final adjustments under Beauregard's critical eye.

Nightingale's suit, I was pleased to see, was a much more traditional shade of black and conventionally cut, although it was tailored very well and suited him perfectly. He was, as one wag back in London once said, dangerously handsome and frustratingly unattainable.

'It's a pity your friend Mr. Gibbs can't be with us,' said Nightingale as he adjusted his bow tie in the mirror.

'They wouldn't let him inside,' I said. 'It's whites only.'

He paused in his adjustments but his eyes never left the mirror.

'Ah,' he said. 'That's a shame. I found him quite interesting.'

I am not by nature a violent man. It's true, I was involved in the usual playful scuffles and occasional fist-icuffs at Oxford and in the aftermath of the Boat Race, but nothing that led to lasting injury. But, by God, I was seized by a sudden urge to take hold of Nightingale and throw him out of the window. He has a reputation, but I was no slouch in the basic *formae* and I was sure that I could have him safely defenestrated before he could formulate a counter-spell.

Beauregard cleared his throat.

'Shall I order the taxi now, sir?' he asked.

'Yes, thank you, Beauregard,' I said, and picked up my cane from the umbrella stand by the door.

'Is that the cane you're bringing?' asked Nightingale.

'What's wrong with this one?'

'It lacks a certain something,' he said.

'Ah,' I said. 'I see.' And went to fetch my cane with the etched steel handle from its carrying case in my wardrobe. This cane has a metal core and is noticeably heavier than my preferred hickory and silver-capped model. When I picked it up I felt a single pure note and a wash of heat that made me shiver. I had paid a pretty penny for this cane, but had never used it to cast so much as a werelight.

Solve the mystery, I said to myself, *and the Nightingale flies home.*

'Gussie,' called Nightingale. 'Our car is here.'

'Right-ho,' I called back.

4

I think it was Charlotte Brontë who once said that it is a truth, universally acknowledged, that a pair of single men in a club must be in want of feminine company. So I was far from surprised when a fine example of the feminine form slipped into the spare seat at our table.

She was a modern American girl, which meant that her hair and dress were scandalously short and her manner forward. She had a handsome profile and slender neck and seemed familiar, but I couldn't place her – although she certainly seemed to know me.

'Why, Gussie,' she cooed. 'Are you going to introduce me to your handsome friend?'

That put me in a quandary, since I couldn't introduce the young lady as I had no recollection of her name. On the other hand, these modern girls are not beyond pretending to familiarity in order to oil their way into one's company, so I bit the bullet and decided to fall back on my upbringing.

'I'm afraid you have me at a disadvantage,' I said stiffly.

'Perhaps I do,' she said with a sly smile. 'You may call

me Cocoa.' She looked over at Nightingale. 'And now you may introduce me.'

Nightingale saved me the job by extending a hand.

'Thomas Nightingale,' he said, and they shook in the rather masculine fashion modern girls seem to prefer.

'Cocoa,' she said again, but the bell of memory remained resolutely un-rung. 'Pleased to meet you, Tommy. Have you been in New York long?'

'I arrived just this morning,' he said.

'My, you do work fast, don't you, Tommy?' She affixed a gasper to the end of a long black holder and pointed it at Nightingale. 'Got a light?'

Nightingale hesitated a moment before drawing a matchbook from his pocket and, with a flourish, lighting a match one-handed. I thought it was damned impressive myself – I've always burnt my fingers when I've attempted that particular trick – but Cocoa seemed less than impressed. Perhaps even disappointed. Still, I don't claim to understand the minds of these modern women.

'What do you think of the band?' she asked Nightingale.

I'd given Nightingale a surreptitious glance during the band's first set. His face had been fixed in a perfectly pleasant expression throughout the first number, and stayed that way even when the band was joined by some very comely coloured showgirls with scandalously short skirts and exposed navels.

The funny thing is that, had I encountered this band in London, I would have thought them very fine indeed. But for all their skill, the musicians stuck to the sort of foxtrot-fixated dance music that one might hear on the wireless. Lucy certainly wouldn't have approved, and I was really quite glad he hadn't been able to attend. He can become quite scathing when he doesn't think the jazz is up to scratch.

'They seem perfectly fine,' said Nightingale.

'They're just the warm-up,' said Cocoa. 'The real stuff is in the next set. Want to dance?'

To my surprise, Nightingale said he would. As the next set commenced, he stood to take Cocoa's arm. She leaned over and winked at me.

'There's a new dance,' she said. 'You'll like this one. It's called the Black Bottom.'

And then, with a gay laugh, off she went, leaving me none the wiser.

Nightingale danced just the way I'd expected him to, with grace and precision but with no sense that he was letting go or losing himself in the music. Lucy dances in his own little world with frequent stops to listen to the band and make, so he tells me, mental notes. He once asked me what I thought of while I was dancing, and I had to confess that I thought of nothing at all – once I'd learnt the steps, that is.

Cocoa took pity on me and, swapping out Nightingale, taught me the Black Bottom, which really wasn't as *risqué* as the name implies. I turn a good leg on the dance floor and soon picked it up, earning, I believe, the respect of Cocoa, who returned us to our table and insisted on ordering champagne at a ruinous price. This was to be expected, and so I signed the chit without demur as the dance floor was cleared, the showgirls returned, and a lady of operatic proportions gave a rendition of 'I've Found a New Baby' in a style of which Ethel Waters would have been proud.

On the second chorus, the singer swept in amongst the tables and paused at ours to exchange conspiratorial looks with Cocoa before gliding on. I turned to ask her whether she knew the singer, but was distracted by the look on Nightingale's face. He was intent on the band, where a young man – coloured, like all the performers – had stood to break into a trumpet solo.

'Do you know him?' Nightingale asked me, but I'd never heard him before. Whoever he was, he was good. But when I listened carefully, I could sense the same thing Nightingale could. Intertwined through his melody was a silent counterpoint, a breezy whisper amongst the treetops, the smell of pine and lazy buzz of a bumblebee. I could almost taste the honey.

'Johnny Black,' said Cocoa. 'New talent up from Memphis.'

'Interesting,' said Nightingale. 'You seem well informed. Do you think Mr. Baker is in the club tonight?'

'I saw him when I came in,' said Cocoa.

Nightingale declared that, in that case, he would go and pay his respects, and stood.

'Why don't you stay here and keep Cocoa entertained?' he said, which I took to mean: keep an eye on the trumpeter while he was away. I was all for this role, not being one for confrontations – particularly with shady nightclub owners – and while the band was not as modern as I might have liked, unlike Lucy, I rarely feel the need to absent myself from poor music. I believe he feels that listening to inferior jazz may contaminate his higher musical sensibility. It comes as a shock to many to find that aficionados of modern music can be quite as snooty as any *habitué* of the Royal Opera House. More so, come to think of some of the rummy types one finds around Covent Garden.

After Nightingale had gone, Cocoa and I sipped the ruinously expensive champagne and watched the show, which was livened up considerably by a pair of male tap dancers who so astonished with their fluid dexterity that it was almost a relief when the chorus girls joined them and they had to slow down so the ladies could keep up.

'Your friend Tommy,' said Cocoa at the end of the set. 'Is he famous, rich, one of those lords?'

'Why do you ask?' I asked, which made her laugh.

'Because you treat him like he is,' she said.

'He was above me at school,' I said.

'Was it a swell school?'

'Was yours?'

'Mine could have been better,' she said. 'But they say you learn all the important lessons outside of school.'

'That's certainly true of Oxford,' I said, for I had many happy memories of learning to drink while balancing on the back of a chair and how to kiss *au français* and other secret skills.

I am not the tallest beanstalk in the kingdom, but by then I had realised that there was something decidedly rummy about Cocoa. She seemed ill at ease, as if waiting for somebody else, and when we finished the champagne she did not chivvy me to immediately buy another bottle. Good sport that I am, I was about to suggest another bottle myself when Nightingale reappeared at the table and said it was time to leave.

I had just enough time to bid adieu to Miss Cocoa before having to race after Nightingale, who was briskly striding out of the club.

'Are we following someone?' I asked when I caught up with him on the street.

'Not yet,' said Nightingale.

Despite what you might see in the cinema, New York is remarkably free of alleys. But there was a mews behind the nightclub where the stage door let out amidst oversized American dustbins and piles of rubbish from the kitchens. A couple of rats squeaked and scampered away as Nightingale drew me into the shadows. Even with the persistent rain, I might have thought the situation had romantic possibilities if I wasn't so sure that we were, in fact, waiting for someone else.

'I ascertained that Mr. Black would be finishing his set by eleven,' said Nightingale. 'When following a target it's always better to be slightly ahead of them at the start. Otherwise, by the time we'd left our seats and come back here, he could have been long gone.'

I understood the logic, but I was still mourning that second bottle of champagne. I was about to give expression to my sense of loss when Nightingale whispered 'Quiet' in my ear and pointed at the mouth of the mews.

A small skinny boy, no more than eleven, dressed in long trousers, puttees, a ragged raincoat and a flat cap, crept in from the street and leant up against the wall. When he turned to look towards the stage door I could see he was coloured. He sighed and hunched his shoulders against the rain, and I didn't need Nightingale to warn me that he, too, had been set to watch the back of the club.

I felt, rather than heard, Nightingale whisper a long complicated spell and experienced a dashed strange sensation, as if the air were thickening around me. I glanced to the left and right and saw that the shadows which concealed us had grown thicker and darker. This was advanced magic indeed, and I was reminded that while anyone can use a violin as a club, not everyone can make it sing.

We waited what seemed half the night before the door banged open, and we watched as half a dozen musicians emerged from the stage door, chatting, laughing and lighting up gaspers. Mr. Black wasn't amongst them, and I was about to step out of our personal shadow when he stuck his head out of the door and looked suspiciously both ways. He then slipped out and cautiously walked to the end of the mews. When I went to follow, Nightingale put his hand on my arm to restrain me. The young boy in the flat cap waited until Mr. Black had passed by before pushing off the wall and following. Only then did Nightingale and I follow suit.

I don't know if you've ever attended Royal Henley, particularly when it rains, but if you have experienced the well-dressed crowds, the bustle and the sheer energy, then I'm here to tell you that Lenox Avenue was just as bustling, only long, straight and with the added

48

risk of being run over by a trolleybus. And although the risk of drowning is much less, it's just as difficult to follow someone through the heaving mass, especially when they know where they are going and you don't. And you don't want them to know you're following them.

'Where do you think he's going?' asked Nightingale as he slid gracefully through the crowd.

'I haven't a clue,' I said, and swerved to avoid a collision with the umbrella of a portly lady of middle years in a large but unfashionable hat. 'I don't suppose we might just ask him?'

Fortunately for us, the young boy in the flat cap proved a dogged pursuer and so, by making sure we kept either him or Mr. Jonathan Black in sight, we successfully tracked our quarry to a basement speakeasy on 135th. A pair of large coloured gentlemen, serving as what the Americans call 'bouncers', eyed us with an air of bemusement as we approached the door. Once inside, it was quickly apparent as to why. Everybody in the establishment, from the barmen to the clientèle to the small band on the stage, were Negroes. This was a club where white men were prohibited.

It is one of the rummy aspects of New York life that many places – clubs, restaurants, and even shops – operate on what they call 'Jim Crow' principles, although as to who Mr. Crow was, neither Beauregard nor Lucy, who between them know all there is to know about everything in America, would provide illumination. Such establishments do not admit coloured people regardless of whether they are the right sort or not, or even if, like the Alexandra, the performers and staff are co-loured. Some Negro club owners reciprocate and refuse to allow in white customers. When I asked Lucy why, he answered that sometimes black folks needed to escape to somewhere where they didn't have to worry about the white man.

When I inquired further whether he felt he needed to escape me, too, he said that yes, on occasion he did. I have to say that I found that dashed rummy, but Lucy said I shouldn't take it personally. It was just one of those things.

I found a nice unobtrusive booth at the side, but try as I might I could not get a waitress to notice me. After a while, a slim coloured man in quite the best suit I'd seen in New York so far slipped in to join us. He had a boxer's face, although I did not think for a minute he'd acquired his lumps and scars in the ring. It was, as the song might say, a face that had seen trouble. When he smiled, there were gold teeth.

'Gentlemen,' he said, 'why are you here?'

'My name is Thomas Nightingale and I'm a talent scout for a London music publisher,' said Nightingale. 'Gussie here said your band was reputed to be top-notch, so I was hoping to listen in.'

The man nodded thoughtfully and then turned to me.

'I've seen you around,' he said. 'You're a friend of Lucien's. Do you vouch for this man here?'

'Absolutely,' I said. 'They're always looking for new faces in the West End – that's the West End of London, which is where the shows—'

The man held up a hand to cut me off.

'I've visited London, Mr. Gussie,' he said. 'I am aware of Theatreland.' He clicked his fingers and a pair of cocktails materialised in front of us. 'You may stay to the end of the set,' he said, and stood up. 'And the drinks are on the house. Enjoy the show.'

Which I did. And, more remarkably, so did Nightingale. This band were the proper stuff, and when Jonathan Black played his solo the notes cascaded and entwined like the wind blowing through musical leaves, a wind that then gathered them in a taut little tornado and swirled them to a swiftly spinning conclusion. Nightingale sat with his eyes wide, but seeing nothing, and I smiled to myself and thought, 'Gussie, old boy, another convert to the cause.' Even the cocktail, which was pure Harlem gin flavoured with limes and sugar, failed to lower the mood, although Nightingale wisely left his untouched.

He sighed when the set ended.

'I think I am beginning to see the attraction of this music,' he said. 'Did you notice the *concordia arcana* behind Mr. Black's solo?'

'Rather,' I said. 'You never said whether Mr. Baker was helpful or not.'

'So I didn't,' said Nightingale. 'How remiss of me. It was quite an interesting conversation, but I think we should seek out our elusive trumpeter before our host becomes restive and throws us out.'

I glanced over to where the well-dressed bruiser stood to one side of the stage, no doubt surveying his domain. He caught my eye and frowned.

'I do have a burning question for him, however,' I said.

The frown deepened as we approached.

'Sir, I wonder if you might satisfy my curiosity in one matter?' I asked.

The man raised a dangerous eyebrow.

'Just the one question?' he asked.

'You must tell me who your tailor is.'

When the chap had stopped laughing, he wrote the name and address on a small notepad and handed it over. I had just enough time to thank him politely before Nightingale got a firm grip on my elbow and guided me into the kitchens.

'Quick,' he said. 'Our quarry is flushed.'

'What makes you think he's going out the back?'

'Because we're not the only ones on his trail.'

We reached the bottom of a dim narrow staircase in time to see Mr. Black pause at the top to shrug into his raincoat and push his way out. Up the steps we trotted, with Nightingale in the lead, and out into the rain. There was another of those unpleasantly rubbish-strewn areas that always lurk behind even the best locales, and a passageway through the buildings opposite that led off to the street.

Mr. Black saw us and turned to leg it up the passageway, but before we could give chase he came running back towards us. Behind him a dashed unpleasant but musical voice called, 'Johnny, Johnny, why are you making this hard for us?'

Mr. Black swung at Nightingale with his trumpet case, but Nightingale avoided the blow easily and caught Mr. Black's arm as casually as if they were dancing. Down the passageway I could see pale faces over cheap suits, walking purposefully towards us.

'Who are your friends, Johnny?' said their leader.

'Gussie,' said Nightingale. 'If you don't mind?'

I did mind, because had I wanted to spend my time rough-housing with riff-raff, ne'er-do-wells and belligerent fae, I would have put myself forward to become a prefect, or whatever it is the likes of Nightingale are calling themselves these days. Nonetheless, never let it be said that an alumni of Casterbrook was ever backwards about rallying round when push comes to shove – or when *impello* comes to *propellare*.

Those are spells, I might add.

Mindful that I didn't relish the thought of the thuggish gentlemen seeking retribution at a later date, I threw a *fulge* in their face to dazzle them and prevent them getting a good look at yours truly. Then, while they staggered around clutching their eyes and shouting, I knocked them down with an *impello palma* – one two three – and then stuck them to the ground with a treaclefoot. Of course, they wouldn't stay down long, but certainly long enough for us to leg it back down the stairs and into the club.

'Very nice,' said Nightingale as I used the wood variant of *ianua adhaeresco* to stick the back door closed.

'Who are you?' asked Mr. Black as we made our way to the street via the kitchens, the pantry and, accompanied by screams of outrage, the ladies' changing room. Eventually we were standing in the rain on 135th Street, trying to restrain our trumpeter while not being too obvious about it.

'We mean you no harm,' said Nightingale, 'but we need to ask you some questions.'

'Are you cops?' he asked.

'No,' said Nightingale. 'We're instrument makers.'

5

As I believe I have mentioned previously, thanks to the efforts of the mysterious Mr. Crow, there are few places coloured and white patrons can gather together in public without drawing attention. Particularly when musically voiced but unspecified thugs are on your trail. So I suppose it was inevitable that we would end up at Lucy's diggings on Sugar Hill, where the well-heeled denizens of Harlem roosted. He rented a basement flat of what the Americans call a townhouse, the upper floors of which were occupied by a family of undertakers. Next door, Lucy has informed me, lives a celebrated physician who specialises in maternity care. Thus, as I believe I have mentioned before, from birth to death, a man may never need to set foot outside Harlem.

'When a man is tired of Harlem,' quoth Lucy, 'he is tired of life.'

Lucy opened the door dressed in an exquisite red silk dressing gown with gold embroidery that I admired tremendously, and not solely because I had purchased it for him as a Christmas present and owned a matching garment in green. Unfortunately, all clothes, be they ever so carefully tailored or pressed, immediately rumpled once Lucy has donned them. I've seen it with my own eyes and the process is essentially instantaneous. I once turned to Beauregard for advice, but all he could offer was that it was sometimes the gentleman's lot to bear such vicissitudes with fortitude.

Fortunately, the dictionary I keep in my desk for such moments had a definition for vicissitude.

Lucy certainly looked as if the vicissitudes of life were pressing heavily when he opened the door to find the three of us on his doorstep. Since he did not keep a valet himself, it fell to me to arrange refreshments in the drawing room while Lucy withdrew to don one of his disreputable tweed suits. Lucy keeps a couple of bottles of my Canadian whisky on hand for visitors or when we entertain select friends. I didn't spare the spirits as I poured the drinks, since we were all in need of a restorative.

Lucy knew Mr. Black by sight and Mr. Black knew Lucy by reputation. All the good musicians of New York knew about Mr. Lucien Gibbs and his incisive reviews in *The Crisis* and *The Messenger*. When I pointed out that many musicians lived in fear of his disapprobation, Lucy smiled, somewhat smugly, and said that they only lived in fear if they feared the truth.

It's a rummy thing, but I could have sworn that what Mr. Black actually feared was his trumpet. There was something odd about the way he gingerly removed it from its case and placed it on an occasional table for our inspection. There's always been something appealingly compact and masculine about the trumpet – if an instrument can be said to have an essence, that is. But this one certainly had an essence, and indeed felt dangerously alive. I could believe that it thought its own thoughts, made up of scales and tones and harmonies. At school we were taught to be wary of such things. They start small but they can grow.

Nightingale, with feigned casualness, reached out a hand to touch the bell and run a finger down the pipe. He looked at me and frowned, and then turned to Mr. Black.

'Tell me, Mr. Black,' he said, 'how this instrument came into your possession.'

'I was hired for an engagement on Long Island,' said Mr. Black.

'Who hired you?'

'Old Fat Sam Milovic who manages the Lenox Avenue Swing Band,' said Mr. Black. 'They were short a trumpet for a private engagement, a party up at some grand place past Manhasset, and I was still building a reputation at that time.'

Mr. Black described the location of the engagement as 'the kind of place I always imagine the King of England owning', and had its own ballroom, even bigger than the Roxy.

'The crowd was nothing but Nordics, so the dancing wasn't much, although some of the white girls were pretty,' said Mr. Black, who'd been warned not to get carried away during his solo. As the bandleader had said, 'These folks won't appreciate your style, boy, so you might as well save it for them that does.'

Still, Mr. Black hadn't been able to resist slipping

some hot licks into the turnaround of 'Don't Bring Lulu'.

'You know how it is,' said Mr. Black. 'If you've got it, you've got to let it out.'

His trumpet apparently agreed, because it now gave a queer sort of harmonic buzz at the words 'let it out'. Mr. Black visibly edged further away from the instrument.

During their break at this engagement, some of the musicians had stepped outside for gaspers and to jazz some muggle, Mr. Black amongst them, although he assured us – and Lucy in particular – that he never did reefer when he was playing.

'Too much respect for the music,' he said. 'Also, I don't like the smell.'

Which is why he had moved away a little to a more isolated spot around the corner of the mansion, when something made him look up.

'It was strange,' he said. 'It wasn't a noise or a light. It was more like a feeling, like I'd heard my name called by someone who wasn't there. So I looked up and saw this face peering out at me from one of the high windows.'

'Pale and sad' is all he could manage as a description.

'Not that I had much time to look,' said Mr. Black.

Because that's when she dropped the trumpet case on him.

'Caught it just in time,' he said. 'Damn near knocked me down.'

When he looked up again the face was gone, and Mr. Black cheesed the case in the staff restroom while they completed the next set. He didn't dare open it until he was back in his diggings and tried it out.

'It was already morning by then,' he said. 'So I went

out on the fire escape and gave it a whirl. I knew it was special from the first blow. So smooth, like silk – know what I'm saying?'

'But?' said Nightingale.

'You can get tired of smooth, can't you?' said Mr. Black, and he stepped further back from his trumpet. 'Real music has those rough edges. Smooth is for liars, fakeloos and preachers, ain't it? It's beautiful, but I don't trust the sound coming out of it any more.'

'Why do you keep the bally thing, then?' I asked.

'I pawned my old trumpet,' he said. 'Now I'm stuck with this one.' He looked at Nightingale. 'It's cursed, ain't it? That's the feeling I get from it. Like it's got some purpose other than music.'

'I rather believe it is,' said Nightingale. 'How much would it cost to redeem your old trumpet?'

My earlobe began to itch as I foresaw – clearly, as it happened – that my ear was about to be severely bitten. In the end I forked out the green – American money is all green, for some reason. But Lucy had to chip in to make up the amount. Enough, in my opinion, for a brand-new trumpet and then some.

'And once you have recovered your old trumpet, I suggest you look for employment in a different city, at least for a year or two,' said Nightingale. He looked over at Lucy. 'Suggestions, Lucien?'

'Chicago?' said Lucy. 'I hear good things about Chicago.'

'There you go,' said Nightingale. 'I'm sure we can arrange a ticket.'

Not without a trip to the bally bank first, I thought.

Nightingale packed the cursed trumpet back in its case, being careful, I noticed, to touch the instrument as little as possible.

'Do you remember who the owner was of the house on Long Island?' he asked.

Mr. Black didn't, but he was sure Fat Sam would know, since he arranged the engagement.

'And once we have the address, what then?' I asked. 'Are we to march up to their door and inquire about enchanted instruments?'

'You know, Gussie old bean,' said Nightingale, 'we might just try that.'

Mr. Black's rented diggings were in a tenement building on 134th Street in the part of Harlem they call the Valley. Lucy says that here the inhabitants are charged twice the price for half the space, because if they move in anywhere else the local Nordics will set fire to their front door. We were visiting, in the rain, because Nightingale believed that the thugs I'd stuck to the pavement were bound to have made it their next stop.

'Two to one they've called it a night,' I said.

'I'll take those odds,' said Nightingale, and for a moment it looked like I might be ten pounds up, except we spotted the skinny coloured boy who'd been watching the alley behind the Alexandra. Hunched in a nearby doorway, he looked like a drowned mouse that had been left guarding the empty cheese store while his friends have all scurried off for an evening of port and Stilton. And he did not look happy at all.

Doubtless his disposition was not improved when

he looked up to find me and Nightingale striding purposefully towards him. And dampened even further as, when as he tried to run, he found his shoes stuck to the ground.

'Good evening,' said Nightingale. 'Were you by any chance keeping a lookout for Mr. Jonathan Black?'

'Are you cops?' asked the boy.

'No,' said Nightingale. 'We're from the lost and found.'

Naturally, it took some time to persuade the boy that we meant him no harm. But, aided by the liberal application of dollar bills – which, I might add, came out of my reserve supply – we were able to elicit the information that he was, indeed, yes sir, keeping an eye out for that trumpet-playing man.

Nightingale asked what procedure the poor drowned boy was to follow in the event of Mr. Black being foolish enough to show his face. The boy said that he was to report his presence to the white men who'd paid him to watch and were even now cheerfully ensconced, warm and dry, in a nearby bar.

'If you would go and fetch them?' said Nightingale. 'And then I believe it might be wise to retire for the night.'

It took the thugs less than five minutes to draw up in two automobiles, during which time the rain intensified. Some of the men alighted and advanced on us, no doubt with a view to laying hands on our persons, but we forestalled them by strolling nonchalantly over to the closest flivver, where their leader had sensibly decided to stay out of the rain.

Nobody had drawn any weapons yet, which was a relief to me and good news for them.

Nightingale held up the trumpet case to show the leader.

'You wouldn't be looking for this, would you?'

When I was at Oxford I thought nothing of rising at dawn, avoiding lectures the livelong day and then commencing a late supper with pals and a night of revelry. Occasionally these nocturnal frolics would end with an early morning jaunt upon the Isis in a borrowed punt. I believe it was a sign of my growing maturity that I no longer relished the prospect of messing about in boats, especially in such disreputable company.

Not that there was anything disreputable about the sixty-foot motor yacht that awaited us over at the docks. In fact, once we – that is, Nightingale, the top thug and I – were seated comfortably in the finely appointed lounge compartment and the yacht cast off, we were offered coffee and pastries.

The top thug was an ugly customer, albeit a well-dressed one, the same blighter with the musical voice that I'd knocked down at the back of the club. His head was shaved at the sides, and his thinning light brown hair had been slicked back above a pair of cold blue eyes, a strong nose and a square jaw which he had a tendency to grind.

We slid through the dark waters with the lights of the wharves gliding past.

'So is this your boat?' I asked brightly.

Now, many will tell you that I have a tendency to

chatter when nervous. And, mindful of this, I did try to maintain the same air of stoic taciturnity as Nightingale throughout the two hours or so we were afloat. But it's bally difficult to keep your nerve stuck on a boat, in the dark with a brace of brunos and heading who knew where?

Long Island, it transpired.

A huge house, larger than Buck House but not as squared off, and blazing with light and music. As we moored at the private dock, it was obvious that a party was underway, or rather had reached that stage when half the guests have left or collapsed and the remainder aimlessly wander in search of a reason to stay awake. We walked past at least one couple *en déshabillé* in the bushes as we were led up a gravel path towards the side of the house.

Nightingale scrutinised the top windows, no doubt thinking of the pale face and the carelessly thrown trumpet case.

We were led in through a side door and through the kitchens, up a flight of uncarpeted wooden stairs, out of a disguised doorway into a vast office with a desk you could play ping-pong on. The top thug showed us to a pair of leather-bound pumpkin-orange chairs facing the desk and, leaving us under the watchful gaze of two of his underlings, left the room.

'I say . . .' I started, but Nightingale waved me to silence.

Behind the desk was a tall window through which we could see the formal gardens leading down to the private pier, and beyond that, the black waters of the bay.

Which bay precisely, I'm not sure. I keep meaning to look it up on a map but for some reason I've never got around to doing so.

But it was definitely a bay. Of which Long Island has a great many.

Somewhere outside, a band was not so much winding up as going down with the ship, and there were occasional shrieks and gales of laughter tinged with desperation. I judged it must have been an excellent night out and wished I hadn't been otherwise engaged.

There was no mistaking the man the top thug returned with as anything less than the big cheese, the lord of the manor and the boss of bosses. A tall languid man of late middle years, with a long neck upon which a round head bobbed like a globe lamp with a face painted on it. Judging from the blotchy cheeks and the bleary gaze he threw at us when he entered, he had been an enthusiastic participant in the night's revelries. His evening suit, however dishevelled, was unmistakably from Henry Poole of Savile Row.

I followed Nightingale's lead and stood politely when he entered – he waved us back down and sat in the leather chair that matched the desk in size and grandeur. A coloured servant entered with a jug of coffee but only, I noticed, a single cup.

We watched as he drank the first cup, and then waited some more as the servant poured a second before being sent out of the room.

The top thug remained.

'Do you know who I am?' asked the man behind the desk.

'I'm afraid you have the advantage of me,' said Nightingale. 'But my name is Thomas Beresford, and this is my associate Bertram Wilberforce. We're musicologists from the Royal College of Music in London.'

Nightingale fished a card from his jacket pocket and held it up. After a pregnant pause, the top thug came forward to retrieve the card and convey it to his boss, who squinted at it and then tossed it down on the green baize desk blotter.

'My name is Charles Jaeger,' he said. 'This is my associate Mr. Clydesdale. What brings you to my house?'

Nightingale lifted the trumpet case and placed it on the desk. He opened it and rotated it to display the contents to Mr. Jaeger.

'I believe you were looking to recover this item,' he said.

Mr. Jaeger was not surprised, which in turn was not surprising, since we'd already discussed the matter with Mr. Clydesdale and no doubt he'd briefed his employer. His eyes flicked from the case to Nightingale and then to me. For all the traces of dissipation on his face, Mr. Jaeger's eyes were a hard, penetrating blue, and I was relieved when the gaze passed back to Nightingale.

'And presumably you are looking for a finder's fee?' he asked.

'No, sir,' said Nightingale. 'My colleague and I are interested in where such instruments originate. We thought you might be able to shed some light in that direction.'

Mr. Jaeger smiled thinly and he sat back in his chair.

'I'm afraid I can't really help you there,' he said in

what would have been a far more affable manner if his eyes hadn't flashed dangerously. Lucy is of the opinion that rich Nordics find it hard to mask their feelings. 'After all,' he says, 'they live in a world where everything revolves around their every desire, so there's little need for them to keep their base emotions hidden.' He's fond of phrases like that. Especially after we'd had dinner with Wallace Thurman, who was a Bolshevik to the core. But in this instance, I'm forced to agree. At least as far as American millionaires are concerned.

His face took on a glazed expression that would be familiar to anyone who's ever confronted a small child with a bag full of stolen apples – then became animated again as he thought of a good excuse.

'It was left behind after one of my wife's parties,' he said. 'We never did find out where it came from.' He turned his attention to his henchman. 'Mr. Clydesdale, if you would show these gentlemen out – and . . . oh, provide them with some remuneration for their exertions.'

To my great surprise, Nightingale, the lion of the rugby pitch, allowed himself to be meekly shown out of the same tradesman's door we'd entered through. Although he did have the cheek to pocket the money proffered with ill grace by Mr. Clydesdale. Outside, the sky ahead was already a silver grey as we were then escorted down a long gravel drive, past a mock Tudor gatehouse, and through a decorative but nonetheless tall and imposing gate. Which was firmly clanged shut behind us.

'I say, Thomas – I don't think that man was telling the truth.'

66

'I believe you may be right,' said Nightingale. He looked around. 'Do you have any idea where we are?'

There was a wide gravelled road running perpendicular to the great house and its grounds. Judging by the lightening of the sky, it ran north–south.

'Somewhere on the north side of Long Island,' I said. 'If we walk south, I believe we should encounter the railway back to the city.'

'Good,' said Nightingale. 'Because I think I would like another word with the Reverend Edwards.'

We'd barely left the gates behind when we chanced upon a Dodge automobile that had clearly come off the lane and put its front wheel in a ditch. Being the good Samaritans that we were, we trotted forward to see if we could be of assistance or, if no one was there to assist, we might borrow their vehicle for a ride back to town.

When I stepped onto the running board and looked in the back, I was startled to find a girl in a white fox-fur wrap curled up asleep in the back seat. When I asked whether she was all right, she uncurled and stretched like a cat. It was then I saw that it was none other than Cocoa, the flapper from the Alexandra, wearing a dress that was even shorter and a great deal more shimmery, with beads and whatnot. I think it was a very dark blue or black, but much to Madame Zaza's later annoyance, I couldn't say. Who is Madame Zaza? We shall come to him – or, more precisely, to one of his creations – later.

She had a smear of red lipstick across her left cheek and a dark patch on her forehead. Her marcel wave had suffered overnight so that a frizzy patch had sprung up at the top like a neglected geranium.

I can sympathise, because I remember my mater's hair frequently did the same on hot summer days. And as my dear old maternal origin would do in those circumstances, Cocoa seized a cloche hat from somewhere about her person and jammed it on her head.

And once her coiffure was suitably hidden, she turned her attention on us.

'Good gracious,' she said once both eyes had focused. 'If it isn't the English boys. What are you doing out here in the sticks?'

'I was about to ask much the same thing,' said Nightingale.

Cocoa idly reached down the front of her dress and tugged at whatever it is modern girls wear underneath to make themselves fashionably flat-chested.

'I was at a party,' she said, and vaguely indicated the direction we ourselves had come from. 'Over there, lots of swells and hooch you wouldn't believe. I meant to glom some bottles on my way out, but I was distracted.'

'Were you there on your own?' I asked, while Nightingale inspected the front of the Dodge where it had gone into the ditch.

'No,' laughed Cocoa. 'I was with Orson, or was it Digby? Or perhaps his name was Clarence. Clarence Fitzwilliam III. I was out with one of them, but I think they found somebody more entertaining.'

'I'm sorry to hear that.'

'Don't be,' said Cocoa. 'Whatever his name was, he turned out to be a flat tyre.'

Ironically, the Dodge's own tyres were perfectly

pressurised. However, it was jammed tight into the ditch. Nightingale called me over and we made a great show of shouting and heaving to disguise the fact that he pushed it back onto the road with *impello*.

Cocoa slithered into the driver's seat before we could stop her.

'Thanks, boys,' she said. 'Can I give you a ride into town?'

New York, like London, is constantly growing, so that in order to reach its heart, one must drive through a series of increasingly frantic building sites. Only, this being America, the activity was larger, louder and more audacious than back home, culminating in the Queensboro Bridge, a span across the East River of such magnificence that it soars over Welfare Island without stopping to let anyone on.

Arriving in Manhattan with the sun behind you flashing off the skyscrapers, you'd have to be a bally stone not to feel a thrill in your heart and wish you could play clarinet. An impulse I entirely blame on George Gershwin – although, word to the wise, do not raise the topic of *Rhapsody in Blue* with Lucy unless you have a spare four or five hours to listen to him complain about cultural theft.

Cocoa was an excellent driver, and we made good time through the awakening streets until she pulled over outside my building.

'What do you plan to do with the car?' asked Nightingale.

'Don't you worry your pretty little face about it,' said Cocoa. 'It'll be jake. I know a guy.'

And with that, she zoomed the Dodge off down the street.

'She knows a guy called Jake?' said Nightingale. 'Or did I misunderstand that?'

'"Jake" means good, all right, spiffing,' I said.

The morning doorman gave us a knowing look as he opened the door for us.

'I see,' said Nightingale. 'Did you notice she made a serious mistake?'

'How so?'

'She never asked you for your address.'

6

Now, many of you might be expecting me to regale you with a tale of how, the following morning, I was ripped untimely from my quilted womb, but in truth the sun was already some distance over the mizzen mast when Beauregard drifted in with the coffee. A pot of coffee, mark you, no doubt anticipating my greater need for revivification.

As I sat sipping, Beauregard floated around the room laying out suitable daywear. Judging by the thick wool and conservative cut of the suit, my valet thought that the afternoon would prove to be unseasonably cold.

I asked after Nightingale and was informed that my guest had risen earlier, gone for a walk, and was currently breakfasting in the dining room. When I joined him I found him eating pancakes and grits.

'I asked for them,' said Nightingale. 'When in Rome . . .'

I've visited Rome and I made sure to have kedgeree, eggs and bacon while I was there. Beauregard, wise to his employer's tastes, served me the same without demur or comment.

Once I'd suitably fortified myself with eggs and the strangely brittle bacon that Americans favour, I asked Nightingale what his plans for the rest of the day might be.

His eyes flicked after Beauregard, who had returned to the kitchen to do whatever it is he does in there.

'I thought we might take a stroll in the park,' he said.

The Folly, the slightly shopworn centre of magic in the British Empire, sits on the south side of a garden square not too dissimilar in size and character to Washington Square, although this being New York, the fountain here was bigger and there was a copy of the Arc de Triomphe sitting opposite the start of Fifth Avenue. It was a blustery overcast day, but mercifully free of rain, and we stood in the lee of that arch and watched the men swarming up the scaffolding on the building site opposite.

'They do like their buildings tall here,' said Nightingale.

'It's the ground,' I said. 'One of Lucien's friends explained it to me once. The ground is very hard in Manhattan, which makes it easier to build these skyscrapers.'

We watched a distant figure walk casually along a girder a hundred feet in the air.

'I wonder what it must be like to be so bold,' he said wistfully, and then his manner changed and became crisp and businesslike. 'This Cocoa woman – she seemed to know you.'

'I thought she was familiar, but I couldn't place her face,' I said.

'And yet she knew where you lived,' he said. 'Have you hosted many salons at your flat?'

Truth be told, I had not. The love that dare not speak its name encourages habits of circumspection, and while I've had Lucien and some of our mutual friends for dinner, you would be hard-pressed to regard *Chez Augustus* as the heart of the city's social whirl.

'I'm certain she's never visited,' I said. But then I wondered if I hadn't seen her talking to Beauregard. Even as I grasped at the memory it seemed increasingly unlikely, so I dismissed it. I've always found that too much introspection can interfere with the important things in life.

'No doubt the mysterious Cocoa will reappear,' said Nightingale. 'Do you believe the trumpet player was telling the truth?'

'Which trumpet player – Jonathan Black or the Reverend Edwards?'

'Mr. Black,' said Nightingale. 'With his tale of strange pale faces dropping horns from on high.'

'It would be a peculiar story to make up,' I said. 'Why not just say he redeemed it in a pawn shop or inherited it from a mad old uncle? That would be a cracking mystery, don't you think? A young man on his uppers receives a mysterious parcel, he opens it to discover a magical trumpet, and suddenly his fortune is made. But at what price?'

'Quite,' said Nightingale. 'Mr. Jaeger's story that it was left behind after one of his bacchanalia seems all too plausible. And yet . . .'

'Quite.'

'I think Mr. Jaeger, Jonathan Black and Miss Cocoa may all be in the nature of a red herring,' said

Nightingale. 'I think it might be time for a stern word with the Reverend Edwards.'

'I say, what for?'

'I think he may have been economical with the *actualité*.'

'Gosh.'

'Precisely.'

'Fancy that,' I said. 'And him a man of God, too.'

Nightingale contemplated the automobiles passing by.

'I say,' he said. 'Which one of these cars is a taxi?'

'That beige one with the check pattern,' I said, and hailed it.

'It would be easier if there were some consistency,' said Nightingale. 'Perhaps they should paint them all a single colour.'

I think it would be fair to say that the Reverend David Edwards was less than delighted to find us once again darkening the entrance to his church. The pews were out, and a lectern had been set up on the stage at the end of the room. A dozen or so men and women in blue robes were milling around while the Reverend Edwards himself pored over sheet music with what I realised must be the choir master. As we advanced upon the stage, we were intercepted by a small energetic woman with an attractively stern face. That is, her face was attractive despite the steely-eyed look of disapproval beneath lowering brows.

Indeed, if you like your women stern and single-minded, then this was definitely the girl for you.

'Can I help you, gentlemen?' she asked in a tone that suggested that she doubted both clauses in the sentence.

'I believe you can,' said Nightingale, and introduced us as musicologists from the Royal Society of Pilgrims. 'We wondered if we might have a moment of the reverend's time?'

'You're not getting any more money out of us,' she said, but weakening under the onslaught of Nightingale's charm, said she would fetch him as soon as he was available.

'You'll have to forgive my wife,' said the Reverend Edwards five minutes later. 'She fears I am too gullible for my own good. Gentlemen, please.' He gestured us into a pew and took his seat on the one in front.

On the stage the choir started up, only to stop again so the choir master could adjust the harmony.

'We wondered if you might clarify a few points about the saxophone,' said Nightingale, and Edwards immediately grew wary again.

'What do you want to know?' he said.

'Mark Harper told us that the saxophone had come from his former business partner – a Mr. Steven Baker. Is he known to you?'

'The Doughman?' said Edwards. 'We all know him. He's the other devil.'

'We've spoken to him,' said Nightingale. 'He claimed to have no knowledge of the instrument.'

Edwards scowled and I presume said something pithy in rebuttal, but I wasn't paying attention because the choir had reached the lively part of their hymn. I can extol the chilly virtues of Bach and Haydn and other

Germans, and I've belted out a chorus of 'All Things Bright and Beautiful' myself in the school choir, although I admit I was mostly thinking ungodly thoughts about Cheesewright Junior in his sports kit at the time. But in my book, even 'Hark! The Herald Angels Sing' is as ashes upon the tongue when compared to the way these coloured American choirs can sing. Only the Welsh could give them a run for their money, and only if they cheered up a bit first.

I think Nightingale and Edwards must have got into one of those heated arguments that consists of both parties whispering so intently that they resemble a pair of tomcats preparing for some *felix et felix* action.

It was perhaps because the choir were hitting notes that would have caused a castrato's eyes to water that I failed to notice that Nightingale had asked me a question until the Reverend Edwards laughed.

'Sorry,' I said. 'I was listening to the wrong thing.'

Which only made Edwards laugh harder.

'*Make a joyful noise unto the Lord, all ye lands,*' he said. And right on cue the choir behind him made such a hallelujah that I almost considered taking up religion again. Fortunately, we children of Albion are made of sterner stuff, so the feeling quickly passed.

'Fine,' said Edwards. 'I will tell you the truth. But only because your friend is closer to God than either of us old sinners.' He gave me a long, appraising look. 'Even if he don't know it himself.'

Lucy says that true musicians always make that mistake – confusing a love of music with spiritual awareness. But I knew better than to make this observation at such a crucial juncture of the conversation.

'Like most songs, it starts with a girl,' said Edwards. 'And her name was Maurelle.'

'That's a lovely name,' I said.

'She came to me at a bar in a week before the Armistice,' said Edwards. 'They knew me there since I'd been visiting every time I got a pass. I used to play for my drinks, and by the end of the war we had a pretty good quartet going. It was liberating, being in France. Over there we were Americans, not Negroes. And she wasn't the first white girl that had sidled up to me in that bar looking for some of that southern syncopation.' He looked at Nightingale. 'You wouldn't know about that, would you now?' Then he looked at me. 'Or maybe you do.'

'Anyhow, this frail was different from the rest. She had an air about her, a glamour, a style that had nothing to do with money or clothes or how she fixed her hair. I thought she was an angel. I was wrong about that, but that night she was an angel. After that, she was never far away. Hell, she turned up in camp, never mind the sentries on the gate. I'd just find her lying on my cot wearing a wicked smile.'

He shook his head.

'But there's nothing the army hates more than a bunch of coloured soldiers having a good time. So they shipped us home as fast as they could get us on the boat. I thought, there's a good memory to leaven out the bad, and tried to slip back into my life. Once you're demobbed, the war can start being like a dream or a nightmare that you had. You learn to stop flinching every time an automobile backfires. You start remembering to say "yes sir" to the white men who would have shit their pants under fire. Then, one day I came home from a session and found her lying in my bed, wearing nothing but that smile.'

'Did she say how she got there?' asked Nightingale.

'She never spoke,' said the Reverend Edwards. 'Not even back in Europe. If she wanted you to know something, she had ways of letting you know. Otherwise,' he shrugged, 'you was in the dark.'

So they shared diggings right on 134th Street. And if any of the respectable people had anything to say about it, Edwards wasn't listening to their opinion. He had music and a girl and a place to sleep, and that seemed like Paradise to him.

'A false paradise, mind you,' he added quickly.

Maurelle had been in Harlem for less than a month when she presented Edwards with the saxophone.

'Why a saxophone?' I asked. 'You were a trumpeter.'

'I don't know,' he said. 'But it had the sweetest sound and I'd played a bit when I was younger, so I knew what to do. And the Lord knows there were enough young buglers running around town at the time. I stood out with a sax, especially once I'd started writing.'

'You wrote your own repertoire?' asked Nightingale.

'Does that surprise you?' said Edwards. 'I'd learned musical notation back in Memphis. In those days you learned three things at Sunday school – the Bible, singing and how to sight-read.'

Things had gone well enough, but the saxophone had begun to worry him.

'Sometimes I weren't too sure who was playing who,' he said. 'There was something ungodly about the whole situation. But when I confronted Maurelle, I could get no sense out of her, and then . . .' He trailed off.

'And then?' asked Nightingale.

'Things couldn't go on. I couldn't bear to play the sax no more. But to give it up, I knew I had to give up music, and that was a hard thing to do. When I was with Maurelle, all I could think of was her. And all she wanted was for me to play. She didn't even care if I got paid or not. Just that I played.' Edwards shook his head. 'It couldn't go on. Something had to give. And then one afternoon I was passing this church and I heard the choir.'

The music had drawn him in and he had met the Reverend Greenway, who was pastor, and found himself confessing the whole sorry story.

'It was his idea to put the sax in hock so I wouldn't be tempted. And he gave me a place to stay so I wouldn't have to go back,' said Edwards. 'Gave me a brand-new calling.'

'So you never saw Maurelle again?' said Nightingale. And dashed if there wasn't a frosty note to the way he said it.

'Yeah,' said Edwards. 'Some kind of war hero, right? But there had been times when she would look at me and I was terrified. Scared me out of my ever-loving mind every time I stopped playing. I knew I had to make a clean break.'

'Was it her teeth?' asked Nightingale.

Edwards, who'd been getting increasingly chummy,

suddenly reared back as if Nightingale had presented him with a live cobra.

'Who the f—k are you?' he said, forgetting he was in church.

'We're concerned citizens,' said Nightingale in a soothing manner. 'These instruments unbalance the world, and our job is to nudge things back to the natural order.'

The Reverend Edwards bristled at this.

'There is no natural order,' he said. 'Only God's order.'

'Quite,' said Nightingale. 'Was it her teeth?'

'And her serpent's tongue,' said Edwards. 'She was marked. I should have seen it from the start.'

All this talk of teeth and tongue had me bamboozled – although, as many of you know, this is a state I have found myself in on a distressingly frequent number of occasions. Still, I had the notion that I should have known what they were talking about. But for the life of me, the old cerebellum was as empty as a biscuit barrel on Boxing Day. Nothing but crumbs.

'Do you know what happened to her?' asked Nightingale.

'No,' said Edwards. 'It was all I could do to keep myself from running back to her, but the Reverend Greenway and Adele kept me safe. Saw me through it. People talk about the power of prayer, but I have felt it here.' He tapped his chest.

I had that horrid feeling that I used to get when I was foolish enough to ask my Uncle Clyde how he was feeling. Without fail, Uncle Clyde – normally a jovial old buffer – would launch into a long description of the regularity of his bowels and the complicated regimen involved in keeping them so. Once he had started, it was no use trying to divert the topic of conversation, no matter what cunning ruse one might employ. An unaccountable number of men fall into this habit. Young and old, rich or poor, and whatever the subject – be it bowels, Bolshevism or, in this case, the love of Jesus Christ our Saviour – there was nothing for it but to nod at suitable moments and then leg it at the first opportunity.

Nightingale, far more ruthless than I, cut the Reverend off in mid-flow with a curt but polite expression of thanks, and was off with me trailing gratefully behind.

'I want a word with the wife,' he said as we reached the foyer. 'Did you see where she went?'

I had not. But no matter, for it turned out the formidable Mrs. Reverend also wanted a word with us and was waiting in ambush outside the church. She had adopted an outside hat and black coat of a severe cut, and was attempting an expression of bland politeness that didn't really suit her.

'Gentlemen, if I might have a word?' she said.

Nightingale raised his hat.

'Mrs. Edwards, I presume?' he said.

'That's right,' she said, and then the veneer of cordiality disappeared. 'What do you want with my husband?'

Nightingale suggested that we find somewhere private to converse, but Mrs. Edwards would have none of it, except that we conduct our conversation on the pavement outside the church while the good people of the Valley hurried past – although a number did stop to gape. I thought I saw a familiar female face amongst a bunch of coloured girls gossiping on the corner, and for a moment I fancied that it was our erstwhile companion on the road, Cocoa. When I looked closer she was clearly a coloured lady, although the resemblance was remarkable. I might have investigated, but Mrs. Edwards' commanding voice dragged my attention back.

'I'll thank you for not bringing your troubles into my Father's church,' she said. 'And staying away from my husband. He's a good man. He doesn't need the likes of you dragging him back down again.'

'We're only interested in his friend Maurelle,' said Nightingale.

'She was no friend of his,' said Mrs. Edwards. 'It was her that led him to drink . . . and worse.' She lowered her voice until we had to lean in to hear her. 'He was sick when he came to us. I nursed him through the shakes, the ranting, and all that mess until he was free of it. And her. So you'll excuse me if I ask you *fine* gentlemen to get the hell away from my husband. There are those that owe me favours, and don't think I won't use them up keeping you away.'

'Do you know what became of her?' asked Nightingale.

'What makes you think that I'd know anything about that?'

'Because you're a careful woman, Mrs. Edwards,' said Nightingale. 'And one who doesn't leave things to chance. So I think you'll have made it your business to know.'

Mrs. Edwards cocked her head to one side and let

a small, satisfied smile leak a little sunshine into our lives.

'Last I knew, she went and put her hooks into that devil Mr. Baker,' she said.

7

'The Doughman has her,' said Nightingale once we were in a taxi and the stern Mrs. Edwards safely well astern. 'Mr. Harper said that. The Doughman – Mr. Baker, it's a fairly obvious pun.'

Even I could see that we would soon be stalking Mr. Baker once more, but I had more important things on my mind. Things that pertained to the future well-being and – let's be honest here – happiness of one Augustus Berrycloth-Young, Esquire and expatriate.

'Why are you so interested in this blasted saxophone?' I asked.

If the question flustered Nightingale, he showed no sign.

'When I showed the saxophone to a friend at the Folly, she grew very upset,' he said. 'She wouldn't tell me why, but I got the strong impression that there was some terrible tragedy involved. Naturally, that prompted me to set out to discover what the story behind the instrument was.'

'And then what?'

Nightingale gave me the most peculiar smile, that

seemed to mix determination, excitement and a sort of distant sadness. Which is, I think you'll agree, a bally lot of work for a single expression to do. I can only manage my expressions to mean one thing at a time. But then, I suppose nobody has ever marked me out as a man of destiny.

'I had the receipt and I remembered that you were sojourning here, so I booked a liner over,' he said.

A cold hand gripped my chest as a horrendous thought surfaced like a submarine stalking an unsuspecting steamer.

'Do the old sticks at the Folly know you are here?' I asked.

'Certainly,' said Nightingale. 'I posted a letter explaining the whole op just as soon as I was safely berthed in New York.'

'You sent them a letter?' I cried, as if struck by torpedoes amidships.

'You think I should have sent a telegram instead?'

'I think it's dashed rummy of you to drag me into your bally investigation, letting me think it was authorised at the highest level,' I said. 'I think it's damned hypocritical of you.'

'This is not about playing pranks on policemen and larks at Goodwood,' said Nightingale with some heat. 'At the heart of this matter, real people may be suffering. And I believe that, as keepers of the secret flame, we have a duty to act.'

'Who do you think is suffering?' I asked, and didn't add, 'apart from myself and Lucy' – who had had extensive plans for the weekend. 'And why do you think that?'

'I don't know,' said Nightingale. 'I only know that the saxophone deeply distressed my friend, and I've never known her to be distressed in such a dire manner before. She made it very clear that she expected me to act.'

'And who is this friend?' I asked, but already the hungry pike of suspicion was nibbling at the brightly coloured lure of my memory. Or do you catch pike with worms? I've never been much of a fisherman. Let us just say that the suspicious pike was damned hungry and leave it at that.

'I'd rather not say,' said Nightingale.

'Wait,' I said, having paused only to bash the pike of suspicion firmly with the mallet of certainty. 'You're not talking about that queer scullery maid at the Folly? The one with all the teeth?'

'Her name,' said Nightingale slowly, 'is Molly.'

'You have me tussling with mobsters, ne'er-do-wells and sarcastic millionaires because of . . .' I was about to say 'a scullery maid' again, but Nightingale's face had taken on a dangerous stillness. 'Of . . . of Molly?'

'Yes,' said Nightingale. 'Will that be a problem?'

There was what the novelists are pleased to call a pregnant pause.

'No, no,' I said. 'I just needed it clarified.'

Once we had arrived at the safety of my flat, I retired pointedly to my room, exchanged my street garments for my green silk dressing gown, and took up station at the window seat. From there I looked over Washington Square, the imitation Arc de Triomphe, and north up Fifth Avenue towards Central Park. Beyond the park was Harlem – and Lucy – and I wanted both. Although, had push come to shove, I would have settled for Lucy.

Still, if life has taught me one thing, it is that not everything one wants will just fall into one's lap. Occasionally one must exert oneself to achieve one's goals, and if this means solving the mystery of the missing mystery girl, then so be it.

Prouver que j'ai raison serait accorder que je puis avoir tort, as Monsieur Chastain, my old French master, and the first of the many unrequited loves of my life, was fond of saying.

Now, chaps who know me will know that I am partial to a good mystery novel. Lucy often loudly laments my choice of reading material. He is forever thrusting the likes of Edith Wharton or Jean Toomer into my hands. So far the only one I've really enjoyed was *This Side of Paradise* by that Fitzgerald chap, although the ending was a touch depressing.

'At least they contain important lessons for how we live our lives,' Lucy had told me more than once.

So it was with some satisfaction that I turned to one of the many lessons taught to me from my close perusal of the works of Christie, Sayers and Hammett. For example: I don't know if you, too, are an aficionado of mystery novels, but at about the halfway mark the detective will refresh his memory of the case. Sometimes the blighters write it down; other times they recount the facts to the hapless sidekick or, if one is not available, the audience.

Item one: The Reverend Edwards met a mysterious girl while serving overseas.

Item the second: The girl, Maurelle, followed him back to Harlem and gave him an enchanted saxophone. For a while all was well, but Edwards began to feel trapped, which his wife says drove him to drink or heroin. He pawns the saxophone and takes up religion.

Item the third: the formidable Mrs. Edwards says that Maurelle 'got her hooks' into Mr. Baker, the club owner. He himself makes no mention of this, but Lloyd Beaumont the pianist remembers a tall pale woman in a veil, wandering around the club and dancing backstage during the sets.

If this frail was anything like Nightingale's alarming scullery maid, then she was definitely what we in the magical trade call a 'fae'. I was taught a long and complicated definition back at school, which I no longer remember, but the gist was that they were like men – or women, in this case – only different. And sometimes inherently magical.

I only remember that much because the subject was taught by Monsieur Chastain, so I paid rather more attention to the subject then I might otherwise have.

At one end were the High Fae, the gentry, who lived in castles, had banquets and placed unbreakable *geasa* on unsuspecting questing knights, who, if they ever existed, were now gone from the land. Less remarkable but more common were the Middle Fae – the brownies, wefkins, boggarts, falloys, ballyhoos and a dozen other types I've forgotten the names of. At the bottom of the pile came the goblins, of which there were a hundred types that nobody cared to learn the names of.

'Unlike Berrycloth-Young here,' Monsieur Chastain

had said, 'the fae do not have to strain or work for their magic. It comes naturally to them. The High Fae are, of course, the most powerful. But one should never under-estimate even the lowliest goblin. Can anyone tell me what goblins are famous for?'

I cannot, but I remember Monsieur Chastain had magnificent hands.

I also remember that Monsieur Chastain spoke of the 'higher' fae possessing certain talents. One was en-chantment – the ability to imbue physical objects with magical power – and a second was the ability to walk 'the faerie roads', allowing them to pass quickly from one location to another.

Maurelle had exhibited both qualities so, *quod eros demonstrandum*, was most likely a superior fae from France or Belgium. Also QED, if I'm using the Latin correctly, she could leave America at any time. Perhaps she liked it here, despite Edwards proving a bust.

Expending that much sheer brain power might have winded a lesser man, but we Berrycloth-Youngs, as I have said before, laugh in the face of intellectual exer-tion. I had an objective: the elusive and mendacious Mr. Baker. Now all I needed was an address.

As if summoned by my thoughts, Beauregard insin-uated himself into the room, bearing another brandy and soda.

'Beauregard?' I said.

'Sir?'

'You're a man of the city,' I said.

'To be completely accurate, sir, I was born and raised in New Orleans,' said Beauregard.

'Oh,' I said. 'I didn't know that.'

'No reason why you should, sir.'

'Decent place?'

'New Orleans?'

'Yes.'

'A trifle hot and somewhat fraught on occasion,' said Beauregard. 'However, I believe that you – and, indeed, Mr. Gibbs – might find it of interest from a musicological point of view.'

The notion of an immediate escape southwards with Lucy was an appealing one, but never let it be said that we Berrycloth-Youngs are not remorselessly single-minded in our pursuit of . . . whatever it is we are supposed to be pursuing at the time. Even if this is merely a good tip for the 4.15 at Newmarket.

'What I meant,' I said, 'is that you are a man who knows what's what in the city, a man with his finger on the pulse, the warp and woof of human affairs.'

'I endeavour to stay abreast of events, sir.'

'So if I were to say to you, for example, could you find the home address of Steven Baker, proprietor of the Alexandra Nightclub, would that be within the scope of your undoubtedly extensive talents?'

'Mr. Baker has a rather fine townhouse on East 18th Street.'

'Good God, Beauregard,' I cried. 'Did you just know that off the top of your head?'

'I have a cousin on my mother's side who was in service with his household,' said Beauregard. 'She left under unfortunate circumstances, so the details have rather stuck in my mind.'

'What kind of unfortunate circumstances?'

'I'd rather not say, sir,' said Beauregard. 'Will sir be venturing out this afternoon?'

'I rather think we will be,' I said. 'Pick out something sturdy, just in case.'

'Very good, sir.'

It was, as Beauregard had noted, a very fine townhouse indeed. Nightingale and I had formulated a plan of action during our walk over from Washington Square. Dutifully, I trotted up the front steps while Nightingale descended into the basement area to try the tradesman's entrance.

I was met at the door by a tall white man in an old-fashioned butler's garb and with an old-fashioned but familiar accent.

'Good afternoon,' he intoned.

'Good afternoon,' I said cheerily. 'I'm here to see Mr. Baker. Is he in?'

'Do you have an appointment?' he said, in tones redolent of the better parts of the old home metropolis.

'I'm afraid not,' I said. 'But it is a matter of some urgency.'

I presented my card to the man, who glanced at it and, no doubt swayed by the superior quality of the card stock and printing, ushered me into the parlour while he inquired after his master's availability.

I have to say it was a very handsome parlour in the modern Deco style, and had I been the kind of chap who kept a notebook, I certainly would have taken notes against furnishing a future flat. I was just admiring a particularly sleek cream-coloured sofa when the screaming started. A short, sharp, masculine yelp of surprise and panic followed by a clattering sound that might have been caused by pots and pans and other kitchenware slamming against a wall with some force, before falling down onto a stone floor.

Beneath the mundane sounds, I could sense the mesmerising metronomic tick-tock of Nightingale's *signare*. He had warned me that it might come to this, so I reluctantly abandoned my admiration of the parlour's furnishings and stepped out into the entrance hall.

I took a grip on my cane, which can be a great comfort to a wizard – not least because it can serve as a blunt instrument in times of need.

There was a sound akin to an elephant hurrying up the back stairs, a cry of alarm, and a florid thickset man in a natty yellow and red embroidered waistcoat burst from a concealed door and into the hall. He slammed the door behind him and only then turned in my direction. At the sight of me, he took a step backwards.

'Get back,' he yelled, his face turning as red as a beetroot.

'Excuse me,' I said. 'Are you Mr. Baker?'

'Get back, damn you,' he shouted, and lunged.

I skipped backwards, ready to cast a spell if need be, but the feller tripped over his own feet without any assistance from me and fell flat on his face. For a second he struggled to stand, but then he slumped back down again, clutching at his nose.

Nightingale appeared in the hallway with the butler behind him.

'Mr. Baker,' said Nightingale. 'You've had a fall. Here, let me help you.'

He gently wrestled Mr. Baker into a sitting position, revealing a surprisingly large amount of blood leaking from his nose. The butler gave a restrained grunt of surprise and stepped forward, only to be met by Nightingale's outstretched hand.

'Some warm water and clean napkins,' he said. 'If you don't mind.'

With my assistance, we helped Mr. Baker into the parlour where, unfortunately, he got blood on his nice clean tan-coloured carpet. We sat him on the Deco sofa and Nightingale solicitously tugged Mr. Baker's hand away and examined his nose. He declared that it was clearly not broken, and handed the poor man his handkerchief to stem the flow.

Throughout these ministrations, Mr. Baker's eyes were wide with fear as he looked first at me, then at Nightingale and back again. At one point they rolled back in his head and I feared he was about to faint. Nightingale can be a fearsome customer, but I couldn't help feeling that this alarm was overdone.

When the butler returned with a bowl, towels and napkins, Nightingale dealt with the injury himself, while shooing the man away to fetch tea and something stronger for his master. Once tea and brandy had been served, Mr. Baker was calmed sufficiently to recover some of his composure, and demanded to know who we were and what we thought we were doing.

'Who did you think we were?' asked Nightingale.

'I have no idea,' said Mr. Baker.

'Then why did you run away?'

'I thought you were assassins,' said Mr. Baker.

'Who would want to assassinate you, and why?'

The question seemed to spark outrage in Mr. Baker, who spluttered that he had made many enemies, so of course he was worth assassinating. How dare we insinuate that he wasn't worth killing? The nerve, the effrontery . . .

'Did you take us for gangsters, then?' asked Nightingale.

Mr. Baker went to shake his head, winced, and gingerly touched his nose. The bleeding had stopped but it had begun to swell.

'No,' he said. 'But there are worse things than honest gangsters in this city.'

'Can you give them a name?'

'I don't know names,' he said. 'I take care not to know names. It's much safer not to know names.'

'I see,' said Nightingale. 'Tell us about Maurelle.'

'Who's that?'

'Purlie Edwards' lover,' said Nightingale. 'The pale quiet woman who I believe stayed with you for a while.'

'Was that her name?'

'So the Reverend Edwards said.'

'*She* never said.' Mr. Baker giggled and caught himself. 'I didn't know.'

'Did she stay with you?'

'Did she f—k my brains out, you mean?' he said. 'Damn right she did. Morning, noon and night. F— king was all she was interested in, except those hinky instruments.'

Mr. Baker's wife had been visiting relatives in the Midwest, or he never would have allowed the situation to develop as it did. As it was, it lasted less than six weeks before Mr. Baker was forced to pass her on.

'When was this?' asked Nightingale.

Five years previously, two years before he'd bought the Alexandra, when he was still in partnership with Mark Harper in Tin Pan Alley.

'How did you meet the Reverend Edwards?' I asked.

Mr. Baker snorted and muttered 'reverend' under his breath. His face had less of the beet vegetable about it, although I noticed his nose retained its ruddy complexion.

'I bought some sheet music off him,' he said.

'Anything I'd have heard of?' I asked, ignoring a quizzical glance from Nightingale.

Mr Baker named a number of titles, several of which I recognised from my dancing days in London. They were all what Lucy might call the tamest sweet dance tunes, and all hits for white performers. Although before I met Lucy, I doubt I would have made such a distinction. Another thing I had learnt from Lucy was how the music business was conducted in America.

'Did you buy the full rights?' I asked.

'Not that it's any business of yours, but yes, obviously. Only a fool publishes anything that he doesn't have exclusive rights to,' said Mr. Baker, with such an air of smugness that I had a most ungentlemanly urge to strike him around the head.

Mr. Baker would have made thousands off that music and paid Edwards a pittance.

'Was Mr. Harper cut in on this deal?' I asked.

'Like I said,' said Mr. Baker, 'only a fool shares any rights he doesn't need to. Mark never rated these coloured composers. He thought they were only good for jigaboo music and minstrel songs. His loss.' Mr. Baker sniffed. 'His loss.'

Nightingale caught my eye and raised an eyebrow. He wanted to know whether I'd quite finished with my detour through the inequities of music publishing. As I believe I have demonstrated previously, Nightingale can make his expressions do a great deal of work.

I opened my hand to indicate that it was his turn on the third degree carousel.

'Now see here, Baker,' he said in his most authoritative voice, which was pretty damned authoritative, I can tell you. 'When Gussie here presented you with my card you immediately attempted to leg it out of the basement. Now, you've never had the pleasure of Gussie's company, but had met me and I had given you my name. So what was it about my name that had you fleeing for your life?'

The confidence that had been returning to Mr. Baker's demeanour drained away, but he said nothing.

'Now, I believe I was perfectly pleasant the last time we met,' said Nightingale, in a tone that strongly implied that alternatives to 'pleasant' could be arranged at short notice. 'And the only thing I asked you about was an enchanted saxophone. So I can only assume that that was the cause of your apprehension.'

Mr. Baker looked blank and then gave me a pleading look.

'Are you scared of us because of the magic saxophone?' I said.

'Not you,' he said. 'I'm scared of what you might bring down on my head.'

8

I won't bore you with a detailed recitation of the rest of the conversation. Nightingale, who on occasion has worked with real police detectives, has told me that effective interrogations are never like what you read about in crime stories. A proper interrogation involves patience and concentration on the part of the questioners – not qualities I am much noted for. Suffice to say, I left most of the hard work to Nightingale while I investigated the contents of Mr. Baker's drinks cabinet and his cigarette box. From these, I learnt two things. One, that the parlour was certainly exclusively for entertaining unwanted guests, and secondly, that no matter how much vermouth you pour in bathtub gin, it tastes like bathtub gin.

Still, when I served it up to Mr. Baker it seemed to lubricate his tongue well enough.

It was the week before Christmas 1921 when Mr. Baker turned Maurelle out on to the street. He had no choice. Not only was his wife of fifteen years returning within days, but the woman had started to show.

'The dumb frail had let that n—r get her basted, so

there was no way I was keeping that around,' said Mr. Baker.

'Truly, you are a prince amongst men,' said Nightingale.

He put the little moocher out of his mind until later the next year, when the bruno known far and wide as 'the Horse' had turned up on his doorstep. A bit of further questioning revealed that this was Mr. Clydesdale of the musical voice, although Mr. Baker didn't know why he was called the Horse. Obviously, the legend of that proud Scottish equine had yet to reach the New World.

The Horse wanted to know where the woman had come from and if she'd made any other instruments, and had he, Mr. Baker, noticed any unusual effects when she attended soirées, clubs or parties?

'I said I'd never taken her to any soirées, nightclubs or parties,' said Mr. Baker, and that was it. For the time being.

The next year, Mr. Baker had bought out the Alexandra and at this point went on a long diatribe, complaining bitterly that Owney 'the Killer' Madden had got the idea of a whites-only Harlem cabaret club from him.

'Bastard used all that hooch dough to buy up the talent for the Cotton Club.'

The Alexandra did OK, though, and provided a steady stream of hopefuls for Mr. Baker's publishing business to exploit. He was going up in the world and could afford the house we were currently sitting in, a genuine English butler and a second, younger, more adventurous wife.

Then the Horse paid him a visit at the club.

'Charles Jaeger sent his compliments and asked that I allow his employees occasional access to the club,' Mr. Baker told us. And of course he acquiesced, because what Charles Jaeger wanted, he got. 'He's in deep with the cops, the DA, the gangsters and bootleggers. Not so deep that he risks a fight, but deep enough that they do him favours. Old money, you know. They walk past you with their noses in the air, but they have their feet in the gutter and they know how to pull the strings.'

But it seemed a small enough burden. Three or four times a month, the Horse would turn up with the woman in tow and she would sit hidden behind the orchestra or in the back.

'You were sure it was Maurelle?' asked Nightingale.

'Who?' asked Mr. Baker, but then, 'Yeah, Purlie's woman. She was wearing a veil but I knew it was her. The way she moved, the way she danced. Like she was listening to music you couldn't hear.'

It seemed an easy, trivial arrangement until Mr. Baker started to notice a disturbing pattern.

'She was a curse,' said Mr. Baker.

It was so subtle, at first he didn't see it. Show business is a fickle enterprise; audiences can be unexpectedly tetchy for no apparent reason, dancers can sprain their ankles or forget their moves, musicians can have a bad night, and you can easily find yourself with a bad batch of booze.

'Especially these days,' I said, thinking of the gin in his drinks cabinet.

The coloured staff complained first, the scrubbers

and the waitresses, and he dismissed their talk of curses as superstition and hoodoo. But as if their complaints had opened his eyes, Mr. Baker began to discern a pattern whereby the bulk of these misfortunes occurred on the nights when the veiled lady was in attendance.

And the problems multiplied and grew worse. Top performers wouldn't even consider the Alexandra, no matter what Mr. Baker offered them. Last year things had come to a head. The Cotton Club had been closed down, and while everybody knew that Owney Madden would shortly grease enough palms to get it reopened, this nevertheless was the Alexandra's chance. Mr. Baker's chance to retake some of that lucrative white downtown trade.

So he told the Horse on the very next visit that he and the Veiled Lady were no longer welcome.

'As you wish,' said the Horse. And the very next day the police raided the club and the Alexandra was shut down for six months.

'But it was worth it,' said Mr. Baker. 'To get rid of that woman.'

And he still lived in fear of the Horse, and of other less easily defined threats.

'I didn't used to believe in hoodoo,' said Mr. Baker. 'But now I know it's real. You can see them witches and hoodoo doctors walking around bold as brass. And another thing – most of them are white, so you can't see them coming.'

'Is that who you thought we were?' asked Nightingale with an amused gleam in his eye. 'Witch doctors?'

'Ain't you?' asked Mr. Baker.

'We're professionals,' said Nightingale. 'Do you know what happened to Maurelle after you exiled her for a second time?'

'I hear she haunts the faggot balls,' said Mr. Baker. 'Nobody gives a shit what happens there.'

Nightingale nodded, thanked Mr. Baker for his time, and it was not until we were safely clear of the house and looking for a cab that he turned to me and asked . . .

'What on earth is a faggot ball?'

Confusingly, faggot, in case you don't know, is a rude American word for homosexuals. So when that word is used, you shouldn't expect a roaring fire or a tasty northern dumpling – or at least, not in the way you may be used to.

'A type of fancy dress ball,' I said. 'A sort of masquerade where people come as themselves.' And then tried to bite my tongue.

'They masquerade as themselves?' asked Nightingale.

'As they might want to dress up once in a while.'

'Do you and Mr. Gibbs attend these events?'

'Many people do,' I said, a trifle evasively, I must admit. 'Many of the top people in the city come to watch the spectacle.'

'Do you happen to know when the next such event is scheduled?'

Such a dangerous question. Of course I did. But I daren't appear too knowledgeable. Then suddenly I conceived of a cunning but subtle wheeze that would dampen suspicion and allow myself to cheese it away from Nightingale. At least for an evening.

'Not off the top of my head,' I said. 'But I'm sure Lucien will know whom to ask.'

'Excellent,' said Nightingale. 'Why don't you contact Mr. Gibbs straight away while I pursue other lines of inquiry.'

'If I must,' I said, and tried to keep the skip out of my step.

Alas, my pleasant evening with Lucy did not get off to a good start, as when I arrived at his flat I found he was already entertaining a number of police officers. I should have noticed the pair of flivvers parked outside, but my thoughts were of *amore*, not *jura*, so the first I knew of it was when I walked in to find Lucy's parlour full of heavyset men in navy blue tunics. One of the brutes popped out of the kitchen as I let myself in.

'Well, look who's here,' he exclaimed in all too happy a fashion.

In the living room I found Lucy sitting on his sofa, sandwiched between two beefy red-faced specimens. He looked wan and stared at me with pleading in his eyes. Sitting in Lucy's reading chair – the high-backed leather monster I had bought him as an anniversary gift because he constantly complained about his back – was a vast corpulent toad of a man, uniform tunic undone to reveal a crisp white shirt straining over his paunch, a glass generously filled with my Canadian whisky in his hand. An open bottle of the same stood on the occasional table beside him.

This was Sergeant Bracknel, and our paths had crossed before. His pink face and squinty blue eyes raised in me an instant desire to belabour him about the head with my cane. Unlike Nightingale's, my expressions are often distressingly obvious, and my anger must have shown because as I stepped forward to confront him I felt one of his constabulary confederates grasp my upper arm in a firm grip.

'Whoa there, boy,' said Sergeant Bracknel. 'You're thinking I won't shoot a white man. But you being a fag, and English to boot, means I wouldn't think twice.' He gave me an unpleasant leer. 'I could always say that your girlfriend here shot you in a jealous rage. Everybody knows how jealous you queens get.'

'Do they?' I said. 'Gosh.'

For some reason, this perfectly anodyne response seemed to anger the lumpen sergeant and caused Lucy to mouth 'Shut the f—k up' at me.

The first time Sergeant Bracknel had busted Lucy and me had been when we were attending a pleasant little concert with friends in a basement speakeasy on Seventh Avenue, although speakeasy was probably far too grand a term for what was clearly someone's parlour. His men kicked down the door, battered the host around the shoulders, and demanded that we empty our wallets. Sergeant Bracknel supervised and intoned that this was an illegal gathering under the Volstead Act and numerous New York City ordinances, but didn't even attempt to make it sound legitimate.

'He must have needed the spinach in a hurry,' Lucy said later. 'Usually he likes to stick around and have some fun first.'

This seems to have been the case, because after a

perfunctory search the coppers made off with the contents of our pockets, but not our watches or the crate of top-quality gin hidden in the cupboard beneath the stairs.

It's a funny thing, but often when some lout commits an outrage on your person – in this case, demanding money with menaces – it can take a peculiarly long time for you to get your dander up. As it was, Sergeant Bracknel had time to walk up the area steps and reach the street before the dam broke, a red mist descended, and I set forth to teach the blighter a lesson he wouldn't forget.

Lucy jumped me and, with the aid of some friends, wrestled me to the ground.

'They're the police,' he hissed. 'There's nothing you can do.'

'We'll see about that,' I exclaimed, but Lucy sat on me and kept talking until the words sank in.

You couldn't fight the police. Dispose of Sergeant Bracknel and he would immediately be replaced by someone new and, probably, worse. In addition, it would be a trivial thing for them to arrest us, beat us and send us to Welfare Island, which apparently was something not to be desired. It was only because they could squeeze us for cash that they restrained themselves from beating us to death.

'You cannot fight back,' said Lucy. 'Unless you want to fight the whole state.'

So I have learnt to keep my temper under control the half a dozen times Bracknel or his ilk have 'shaken us down', as they say in New York. I have buttoned up my rage and kept my counsel in the face of extreme provocation, which is, I might say, one of the principal skills one acquires at a British public school.

And now here we were with Bracknel again.

I didn't think the evening could get any worse until one of the police officers returned with the dress. It was a magnificent dress in blue chiffon, cut knee-length and sleeveless in the modern style, with clusters of beads and silver thread sewn in flowing geometric patterns. It was the work of the legendary Madame Zaza and it, along with the shoes, had cost me an eye-watering sum.

Sergeant Bracknel seized the dress and, leaping to his feet, held it up to his neck as if trying it in front of a mirror. His free hand stroked the fabric with an unpleasant lasciviousness and his eyes lit up with a strange glee.

'Oh, isn't this lovely,' he said. 'This must have cost a pretty penny – too much for a boy like Lucy to afford. There are girls down on Fifth Avenue who would get on their knees for a dress like this.' He turned to wink at his uniformed cronies, who dutifully laughed. 'And I don't mean to pray, either.'

He frowned and looked from me to Lucy.

'Wait,' he said. 'This isn't for him, is it?' He advanced upon me with the dress thrust out, like a wardrobe mistress sizing up an understudy. With exaggerated delicacy he proffered it to me and stepped back as I held the straps to my shoulders.

The dress was a perfect fit. Of course it was.

'So now we know who is the lady of the house,' he

said and, coming close, leered into my face. 'Got the jungle fever, do you?'

Now, as has been elucidated *ad nauseam*, I am not the brainiest of chaps. But I was suddenly filled with an icy certainty that, rather than a routine bust, this particular visit was a different kind of business altogether. This was an act of intimidation. But to what purpose?

'Maybe,' said Bracknel, standing even closer, 'you should give us a show.'

He ran a hand down the length of the dress, smoothing it against my chest, waist and hip.

Then, to make this a true red letter day for the Berrycloth-Young bean, I had a second awful realisation. Bracknel was jealous. He wanted the dress for himself.

'What is it you really want?' I asked.

Now, whether Bracknel took my first or second meaning, I do not know. But it was enough to make him pull away and leave me with the dress. One of his men tittered nervously like a schoolboy toadying to an older boy, which earned him a glare from his superior. When Bracknel turned back to me, all trace of his hitherto gay, playful humour had vanished. He was all business.

'You've been poking your nose in matters that don't concern you,' he said. 'Do it again and we'll cut your nose off.' He glanced at Lucy. 'Or something worse. Am I making myself clear?'

I told him, croakily, that he was perfectly clear. After which he left, but not before trousering all the good booze and spare cash he could find. He left the dress, thank God, and had seemingly overlooked the matching shoes, still in their box in Lucy's wardrobe.

I stood in the centre of the room and shook with impotent rage while Lucy ensured the front door was locked and bolted. Then he put his arms around me until the shaking subsided.

I had to clench my teeth to keep from howling.

'I know,' said Lucy. 'I know.'

I was about to suggest that we should rehang the dress before it got crumpled when a young coloured woman came storming into the living room, brandishing a revolver.

'I swear,' she said, 'one day I'm going to lure that motherf—ker out to the docks and put him in the East River.' She casually dropped the revolver on the mantelpiece next to the ormolu clock and smiled at me. 'Gussie,' she said. 'Where's your ritzy friend?'

There was something dashed familiar about her face. The smile in particular.

'Do I know you?' I asked.

'This is my cousin Amelia,' said Lucy. 'You remember her from New Year's Eve?'

'Only in fragments,' which I thought was both clever and funny, and I would have elaborated on the joke if the swiftly moving omnibus of recognition hadn't unexpectedly turned the corner of memory and struck me forcibly in the ribs.

Her complexion was a shade darker and her eyes larger, but she was unmistakably the white girl who'd sidled up to us at the Alexandra and driven us home from Long Island.

'Cocoa,' I said.

'Really, Lucy, did you have to choose such a slow

man to share your fast life?' she said.

'He can do magic,' said Lucy.

'Can he?' said Amelia. 'That would explain some things.'

'But . . . ?' I said, which I admit lacked a certain *je ne sais quoi*, but luckily Amelia got the gist.

'I am a chameleon, Gussie,' said Amelia. 'Like Dr. Jekyll, I transform into a hideous monster who prowls the nightclubs searching for my prey. Do you read *Weird Tales*? Since you do magic, I would have thought it an appropriate entertainment.'

'She passes,' said Lucy, which left me no wiser than before.

Now you'd have thought, my bean being famously deficient, that two staggering insights within the space of an hour would be enough. But, listening to Amelia – née Cocoa – chattering on about her magazine reading, it occurred to me that her reaction to learning I could do magic had been wrong. If she believed Lucy, she should have asked for a demonstration, and if she didn't – or thought he meant stage magic – she should have still asked for a demonstration, or at least proof. Her incurious response was, well, not to belabour the point, curious.

I would have laid odds of three to one that Amelia already knew all about the magic, probably all about Nightingale and me. Ha. That's what the business with the gasper at the Alexandra had been all about. She'd obviously been hoping that a flash cove like Nightingale would give himself away by lighting it by magic. Fat chance of that.

This intelligence would have to be passed on to Nightingale. But right then I needed a reviving beverage. Fortunately, the original owner of the flat had been a smuggler or a revolutionary or an anarchist, or all three, and had installed a false wall in the pantry with quite a commodious store hidden behind. Commodious enough for Amelia to hide in when the police arrived for tea and intimidation, and with sufficient additional space to stock a demijohn of Harlem gin. I prepared a jug, pouring plenty of lime and soda to smother the taste, and we all sat down in the living room like civilised people to recover our nerves.

Once I was recovered enough to face the prospect of speaking to Nightingale, I called my flat on Lucy's telephone. When Beauregard answered he informed me that Master Nightingale had returned for a light afternoon tea and a change of clothes before heading out once more.

'Did he say where he was going?'

'I'm afraid he did not see fit to confide in me, sir,' said Beauregard. 'However, he did ask me from which station he might catch a train to Manhasset Station.'

'Is that on Long Island?'

'I believe so, sir.'

'And how was he attired for this outing?'

'A rather fetching pair of sporting plus-fours, unfortunately matched with somewhat drab gaiters, boots, and a coat which at best could be called utilitarian.'

'Was he armed?'

'Only with a pistol, sir,' said Beauregard. 'A Webley

Self-Loading Mark One, if I'm not mistaken, worn high on the chest in a gunner's holster.'

'Concealed under the coat?'

'Of course, sir.'

'Thank you, Beauregard.'

'Will sir be returning tonight?'

'No, I shall be bunking down at Lucien's,' I said. 'The rest of the evening is your own.'

'Thank you, sir,' said Beauregard.

I returned to the others and conveyed only that Nightingale had stepped out for the evening.

'Did he say where he was going?' asked Amelia.

I told her I was afraid not, which appeared to vex her, although she put on a brave face. Suspiciously, soon afterwards she gathered her coat and bid us a good night. I sat on the sofa next to Lucy and he put his head on my shoulder.

'Nightingale wanted to know what a faggot ball was,' I said, which made Lucy chuckle.

'Good God,' he said suddenly. 'You don't think he plans to attend?'

'I'm hoping we will be done with this business before Saturday.'

'Let's hope so.'

Lucy entwined his fingers in mine and raised my hand to kiss the back.

'Madame Zaza will never forgive us if we don't wear that dress,' he said.

Nightingale arrived early the next morning, cruelly interrupting Lucy and me as we were enjoying a pleasant and well-earned sojourn in bed.

'Good, you're still here,' said Nightingale as he swept into the hallway. As described by Beauregard last night, he was dressed for shooting or fishing or some other equally rural pursuit, in plus-fours and a khaki jacket festooned with pockets, and sporting a leather knapsack.

He divested himself of his jacket and stared down at the mud which encrusted his boots and gaiters. Sighing, he sat on the ornamental bench by the coat rack and began to unlace himself.

'Mr. Gibbs,' he said, 'I couldn't trouble you for a clothes brush, could I?'

Now I knew that Lucy owned a complete set of clothes brushes and all the other accoutrements that a gentlemen needs to maintain proper standards of dress, because they'd been a Valentine's gift the previous February. And perhaps one day he will trouble himself to use them. Still, they came in useful that morning.

The pristine nature of the brush Lucy handed him was not lost on Nightingale.

'It almost seems a shame to get it dirty,' he said, while I laid down old newspaper to catch the mud.

'How was Long Island?' asked Lucy.

'Frustrating,' said Nightingale. 'I have encountered military bases with fewer sentries, although I did manage to get close enough to meet our mysterious Maurelle.'

Despite the high wall, the gate and the regular patrols, it had been much easier than Nightingale had initially expected. Around sunset he'd spotted a lone female figure wandering the perimeter of the grounds. There seemed to be no guards or other attendants trailing her, so Nightingale had made an estimate of speed and direction of travel and risked scaling the walls at a point where trees created convenient cover on both sides. He'd jumped down, only to find her waiting for him.

'Gave me a start,' said Nightingale, 'I can tell you.'

'And?' I asked.

'She's definitely a fae of some kind. Tall, slender, plenty of teeth.'

'The same as your friend Molly?'

'Similar,' said Nightingale. 'A different tribe perhaps, or clan, or nation. We still don't know how they organise themselves.'

'Hasn't your friend told you?' I asked, but Nightingale ignored me.

'We communicated after a fashion,' he said. 'I believe I conveyed the notion that she should flee with me on the instant, but she was reluctant. Kept looking back at the house, to me and back again. Then she shook her head and fled back to the house. I would have gone after her, only a patrol was approaching and I was forced to retreat.'

He critically examined the boot he was holding before placing it carefully on the paper and moving on to the next one.

'This is what I don't understand,' he said. 'If I could make it over that wall, so could she. If she could travel across the Atlantic to be with Purlie Edwards, then surely she could travel the other way to escape.'

'Perhaps she's not dissatisfied with her situation,' I said.

'That was not my impression.'

'Perhaps Jaeger has something on her,' said Lucy. 'Something she couldn't abandon'

'What are you thinking?' asked Nightingale, who, having finished brushing his boots, stood up.

'Gussie told me that Baker said that Purlie had got her basted,' said Lucy. 'What if there's a child?'

We repaired to the kitchen, where I made tea using the leaves I import at almost as ruinous a cost as my booze. Although at least Sergeant Bracknel wouldn't think to confiscate this.

'It's a possibility,' said Nightingale. 'And it would certainly explain why she wouldn't leave the estate.'

'I thought fae were not attached to their progeny,' I said. Certainly Monsieur Chastain of the beautiful hands had taught me that. The denizens of the *demimonde* – particularly the fae – could be distinguished from civilised men by this very lack of filial loyalty.

'I'm afraid a great deal of what we were taught at Casterbrook about the *demi-monde* and the wider world was wrong,' said Nightingale. 'It is entirely possible that Maurelle might be attached to her child. If there is one.'

'You think Baker lied?' I asked.

'Only if he was opening and closing his mouth,' said Lucy.

'Or just ignorant,' said Nightingale.

'That, too,' said Lucy, and the two exchanged smiles.

'Certainly I will need more solid intelligence before we mount a raid on Mr. Jaeger's estate,' said Nightingale.

'A raid!' I'll admit I said this more as a squeak than an exclamation.

'Did you discover when the next of these "faggot balls" is taking place?'

'Tomorrow night,' said Lucy. 'It's the Spring Masquerade at the Roxy Ballroom.'

'Do you think she'll attend?' I asked.

'It's the biggest drag ball other than the Hamilton Lodge Ball, and that's been and gone,' said Lucy, while not mentioning that so had we.

'Yes, but to what purpose is her attendance?' I asked. I knew why Lucy and I attended, I knew why the downtown gawpers attended, but it seemed dashed odd to me that an obviously powerful fae would gain anything from the experience.

'Presumably the same purpose as her visits to the Alexandra,' said Nightingale. 'Why at this moment is not important. We shall work on the assumption that on Saturday night she will be away from the Jaeger estate.

As will, I suspect, Mr. Clydesdale and a number of Mr. Jaeger's retainers. If there is a child held there, that would be the moment to rescue it.'

'Are you seriously suggesting that we mount a raid on the estate of one of the most powerful men in New York?' The squeak had, distressingly, returned to my voice.

'Of course not,' said Nightingale. 'I will stage that rescue. Your mission will be to liberate Maurelle from her handlers at the ball.'

'No,' said Lucy with some force. 'Assuming you survive, you will be quickly on a steamer back to England. But if Gussie and I are in any way implicated in this . . . this kidnap . . . we will face terrible retribution. Gussie is too good-hearted and too obedient to refuse, but I will not let you drag him into this reckless folly.' Nightingale's faint smile only served to incense him further. 'Do you find me amusing, sir?'

'No,' said Nightingale. 'You're right, of course. It would be churlish to expose Gussie so. If need be I can handle both rescues. I ask only for a safe haven for Maurelle and, if there is one, her child. The flat on Washington Square would serve admirably.'

'And if he refuses?' said Lucy, glancing at me.

'Understand this, gentlemen,' said Nightingale. 'I will attempt this rescue with or without your help. I will leave it to your consciences as to how much assistance you might care to render. But at the very least, I beg your help ascertaining whether there is a child or not. Is there a city hospital that she might have attended?'

Lucy sat back and folded his arms and kept a suspicious eye on Nightingale.

'Of course,' I said. 'A girl like that would have stood out. What with the teeth and all.'

'You keep mentioning the teeth,' said Lucy. 'What on earth is wrong with her teeth?' His lively curiosity had obviously overruled his attempt at stern disapproval.

'It's difficult to say,' I said. 'If they're anything like Thomas's friend Molly, then they will be perfectly respectable in many respects – very white, very even ... Only when she smiles, there seem to be a greater number of them than one might expect, and they're ... sharper.'

'She has fangs?' asked Lucy.

'Fangs might be overstating the matter,' I said.

'If ...' Nightingale hesitated and then continued. 'If I am to attempt a rescue on Saturday, we need to confirm the child's existence before the ball. Preferably today.'

'I don't see how that's possible,' I said.

'Midwives,' said Lucy suddenly. 'I doubt Mr. Jaeger would have delivered the baby himself.'

'A house that big will have maids,' said Nightingale. 'Housekeepers.'

'We don't know where the child was born,' said Lucy. 'But if it was in the city, then chances are there will have been a midwife.'

'If there was a midwife ...' said Nightingale. 'There must have been thousands of midwives working in the city six years ago. I assume they're registered, but even if we could obtain that register and started checking its members, that sort of investigation can take weeks, months to complete.'

'But this is a juicy secret, a strange and wonderful story to tell your workmates,' said Lucy. 'I'm a reporter. Take it from me. The midwives will know.'

'But how do we get them to tell us?' I asked.

'I don't know how it goes in old London town,' he said. 'But here in Harlem we go to the fountain-head of all gossip – A'Lelia Walker, the Queen of Joy herself.'

A'Lelia Walker had a swanky apartment on Edgecombe Avenue and a country mansion in some village north of Yonkers. But her preferred party venue was a pair of Georgian townhouses knocked into one on West 136th Street. The ground floor housed the commodious Walker Hair Parlor, source of a city's worth of gossip, and in the basement was the Lelia College of Beauty Culture, where the next generation of Walker Company beauticians were trained in the arcane science of coloured women's hair treatments.

It was this business, founded by her mother, that was the source of A'Lelia Walker's wealth.

'But not her power,' Amelia was to tell me later. 'Definitely not her power.'

She was famous for her parties, whose guest list included Harlem poets and Wall Street bankers, hustlers, artists and, famously, a prince of Sweden who, presumably, gave her what she was needin'. Although what A'Lelia Walker might be needing, given her wealth, boggles the mind.

Lucy says that he knows what she wanted, but refuses, most unfairly, to tell me.

At these parties, princes, paupers and everybody in between would be rammed into the top three floors of the townhouse like sardines in a tin. Provided you liked your sardines marinated in alcohol, that is.

Lucy has a standing invitation, but we only went once and because we were late we couldn't even get inside. Mrs. Walker was good enough to furnish refreshments to those of us stranded outside, but we both decided that we preferred somewhere where the music wasn't drowned out by the crowd.

A'Lelia received us, appropriately enough, in the music room, while all around us servants cleared away the debris of the previous night. We'd been lucky to find the house vacant. Some of the parties there could last for days. When we entered, the room had been empty save for a grand piano, but three modern dining chairs were brought in and placed in a row behind us. No sooner had we sat than the great dame herself swept in and we all sprang to our feet.

Dancing – or rather, slinking – in attendance was none other than Amelia.

A'Lelia Walker was definitely the kind of statuesque beauty that the old Italian painters favoured when depicting Juno reclining with attendant cherubs. Although this beauty eschewed the traditional rumpled sheet in favour of a severe high-necked dress in dark green and a matching silver-green turban. She had a rounded pleasant face that looked the sort to light up when pleased to see one. But there was none of that beneficence for us.

Instead, her dark eyes swept us up and down while her expression remained that of a woman who has returned home from church to find her parlour full of encyclopaedia salesmen.

'You must be the famous Thomas Nightingale,' she said. 'Sit, sit. Lucien and Augustus we know, of course.'

We sat, but she remained standing, as did Amelia.

'You all know my secretary Amelia,' she said. 'Now, gentlemen. What is it you are here for?'

Nightingale outlined our situation, and while he omitted references to enchantment and magic, I gained the strongest impression that Lady A'Lelia knew enough to read between the lines. Certainly she didn't ask why the saxophone was important or what was special about Maurelle. When Nightingale had finished, Lady A'Lelia turned to Amelia, who shrugged.

'This is New York, Mr. Nightingale. We do things our own way here,' she said. 'We allow Gussie to stay because he's entertaining and mostly harmless. But you have quickly worn out your welcome. There's a balance between the seen and the unseen worlds, which you have already upset. There are men in Virginia, Philadelphia and Washington who are opposed to coloured people taking any control for themselves. So far we have deafened them with jazz and dazzled them with dancing girls. But should they come against us . . .'

Lady A'Lelia shrugged.

'Let us just say it would be better if you caught the next steamer home.'

'Nothing would please me more, ma'am,' said Nightingale. 'But not without seeing Maurelle safe first.'

'There are thousands of females kept in bondage in your own Empire,' said A'Lelia. 'Perhaps your lofty principles would be better applied there.'

'You mistake me, ma'am,' said Nightingale. 'I am not acting out of principle. A dear friend has asked me to act because she cannot. My motives are entirely personal.'

'I see,' said Lady A'Lelia. 'That I can appreciate at least. Still, the SS *De Grasse* is sailing for Le Havre first thing Monday. I suggest you make sure you're aboard.'

'And if I am not?' asked Nightingale.

'Then I will inform the Virginians you are here,' said Lady A'Lelia. 'That should serve as a distraction. And if you are as half as good as your reputation suggests, it will thin out their ranks.'

Amelia gave a peculiarly low and unfeminine chuckle.

'I didn't come here to start a war,' said Nightingale.

'It's your choice, Mr. Nightingale,' she said. 'But if it will speed you on your way . . .' She looked at Amelia again. 'Do you think the wise women will be having a party tonight?'

'It's a Friday, ain't it?' said Amelia. 'What do you think?'

As Amelia explained it to me, because the landlords knew that the coloured folk couldn't get lodgings in the white neighbourhoods, they could charge more than twice the normal rent. Since coloured folk mostly got paid half of what a white worker got, people in Harlem were nearly always short on the rent. To bridge the gap, the good citizens of Harlem had taken to holding rent parties in which private homes were turned into temporary nightclubs, at 25 cents per guest. Cram enough people in, sell enough hooch and enough food and, even after expenses and paying the entertainment, you could clear a month's rent, maybe two.

'The wise women will be having a party, no question,' Amelia assured me. 'There'll be hundreds of rent parties tonight. We just need to find the right one.'

We, in this instance, meant Amelia and I on our own. Lucy had first called upon his physician neighbour, to no avail, before heading off with Nightingale to do a tour of the city hospitals on the off chance they might 'find a lead', as the mystery novels frequently say.

'And better that the Nightingale is elsewhere for this,' said Amelia. 'I guarantee where we're going, a man like that walks in the front door, everybody we want to talk to will be out down the fire escape.'

Now, I've never been accused of excessive pride, but I couldn't help but be miffed at the implications.

'I suppose nobody rates me as a threat at all,' I said, which sounded bally silly to my own ears even as I said it.

'No, they don't,' she said. 'But everybody's genuinely pleased to see you. And for a rich, white Englishman, that's a remarkable feat – don't you think?'

'How do we find the right party?' I asked as we turned off the great wide boulevard of Seventh Avenue on to a narrow crosstown street.

'The invitations,' said Amelia.

There was no point having a rent party if people didn't turn up. And furthermore, you needed people who would pay the 25-cent entrance fee. That did not include your friends and relatives, who would expect to mooch in for free. To bring in the numbers, Harlemites would print up cards advertising the party and leave them attached to the elevator cages and shop windows, or hand them out on Lenox Avenue.

Find the right invitation card and we would find the party we were looking for.

'Now we could run around all over town,' said Amelia, 'picking up as many cards as we can and hoping we will find the right one. Or . . .'

We came to a halt by a hand-drawn cart, one of the many that plied their trade along the street, sharpening knives, fixing pans or buying or selling scrap. This one had a mechanical whatnot with a large handle. Bent over the machine was a shabbily dressed white man with his coat off and sleeves rolled up to reveal ink-stained hands and forearms.

'Howdy, Jack,' said Amelia. 'Can I have a look at the samples?'

Or you could track down the famous Wayside Printer, who just about printed all the invites, and ask to see the samples he kept aside from every job. He seemed to know Amelia well, and handed over a wooden fruit box half filled with brightly coloured cards. She thrust the box into my hands and started sorting through them.

They were a gay collection of invitations, although I did wonder if there were any railway men involved in the *Railway Man's Ball – at Candy's Place,* or whether any card games would figure in the SOCIAL WHIST PARTY given by *Penny and Epps* and offering *Good Food* and *Refreshments*. In fact, there were a number of cards that featured a *Social Whist Party*, and I began to conceive that there might be further hidden meaning contained in the wording. I expressed this to Amelia, who laughed and said that for coloured folks there was always another meaning to everything.

'Here's one for you,' she said, and held up a pink card that read *MR. JELLY ROLL; the boys are back in town. Refreshment, Dancing, Company.*

'I'm not sure I understand what you're getting at.'

Amelia tossed the card into the box.

'You'd better ask Lucy about that one,' she said, and resumed her rummaging. Soon afterwards she held up a card on yellow stock with *BABY IS AS BABY DOES; put your mind at ease with the old bone.* Then an address on West 117th Street.

'Now we're trucking,' said Amelia.

Since she was insistent that nobody who is anybody arrives at a rent party before midnight, I took leave of her and headed back to the flat. I keep a change of necessaries and at least two shirts at Lucy's, but wearing the same suit on consecutive days seemed a wholly unnecessary mortification. The flat was mercifully devoid of Nightingales and Beauregard assured me that there had been no callers, especially those of a constabulary persuasion.

A bath, a nap, a light supper and finally a phone call from Lucy in Queens, where they were checking the local maternity hospital. I informed him of my plans and that I would return to his flat once our business was done.

'Take care,' he said. 'Don't let Amelia lead you astray.'

I didn't need the beautiful hands of Monsieur Chastain to know something was rummy about this particular rent party. There were rather more females than I was expecting, and the men that were in attendance stood against the walls or congregated in the out-of-the-way corners of the room. The women danced with each other to a slow – almost funereal – trombone solo, while somewhere in the darkness a hand drummer was beating out a steady pulsing rhythm. The air was heavy with sweat and perfume, fried chicken and tobacco smoke, bathtub gin and neediness.

There was no doubt that I had stepped deep into the *demi-monde*, and I hardly needed Amelia's hissed instructions to keep quiet and follow her lead.

Amelia had picked me up at Washington Square in a flivver she said she'd borrowed from Wall Street. Just to be safe, we left it on St. Nicholas Avenue where someone was, according to Amelia, bound to borrow it again. Thence to the address, where we'd negotiated five flights of stairs although we could hear the party from the ground floor up.

'Are all these ladies midwives?' I asked.

'Look closer,' said Amelia. 'Tell me what you see.'

I have to say that there are certain aspects of femininity that I admit to being less than familiar with – shall we say, the earthier, more family-orientated aspects? But even I could see that some of what I'd taken for stoutness was something else entirely.

'I see,' I said. 'Many of these ladies are . . . um, ah . . . with child.'

'Well done, Gussie,' said Amelia. 'They bring food, money, occasionally jewellery as a down payment on a safe delivery.'

'Offerings,' I said. 'But to whom?'

'I suppose you could say the midwives,' said Amelia. 'In a collective sort of way.'

'Does it work?'

Amelia shrugged. 'Who knows?'

I was about to ask whether we were any closer to our goal when a round lady in a teal shift slid up to us, and before I could stop her she put her bare brown arms around my neck and kissed me on the lips.

'Who's this?' she asked Amelia.

'This is Gussie,' said Amelia. 'Lucien's gentleman.'

To my great relief, the lady let go of my neck and stepped back to give me the old up and down while clucking her tongue. I'm flattered to say, with approval.

'I birthed him, you know,' she said. 'Lucky Lucien, came out easy, his mama hardly felt a thing.' She gave me an affectionate pat on the cheek. 'Still Lucky now.' The lady turned suddenly to Amelia and, seizing both her hands, pulled her close so that the girl was pressed against the woman's ample bosom.

'What is it you want?' she said. 'Don't tell me you're in the family way?'

Amelia put her arms around the woman's waist and began to dance, swaying against the older woman to the long, slow slide of the trombone.

'I want a story, Aunty,' she said.

'What kind of story, Baby?'

'The one about a special princess who fell into wicked company.'

'What kind of wicked company?'

'The trumpet-playing soldier boy kind.'

'That wicked, eh?'

'The worst. But he's not important to the story.'

'Since you're asking me for this story, I'm going to say the man was a little bit important.' The woman Amelia called Aunty caught my eye and winked. 'If only in passing.'

'So in despair the princess fell in with the wicked Baron of the Gold Coast, who locked her in a tower.'

'That wicked old white man,' said Aunty. 'Shame.'

'But we don't know whether the princess had a child or not.'

'What kind of fairy story is that?'

'The kind we ain't finished with yet,' said Amelia. 'You wouldn't have heard a piece of that story, would you, Aunty?'

'There's a child,' said Aunty. 'A beautiful child with skin like old ivory and hair like a wire brush. They dragged me all the way out to Nassau County and that big ugly house. They knew I was the best, but even so, it was close. Princess or kitchen mechanic, they all holler the same when the time comes, and this one was a biter. Damn near took my fingers off when I tried to reason with her. The poor child was presenting face down and it took me five hours to coax her out. She came out yelling, too. Didn't wait for me to smack her.'

Amelia stopped dancing and stood away from Aunty, her eyes searching the woman's face.

'Do you reckon she's still alive?'

'I do,' said Aunty. 'But you might want to leave her where she is. She's going to need some powerful protection to make her way in the world.'

'Why's that?'

'She had eyes like a goat,' said Aunty. 'Scared the shit out of me when I saw them the first time. Devil's eyes.'

10

'And what do you have planned for this evening?' I asked Beauregard as he laid out a light afternoon repast for myself and Nightingale in the dining room.

'I thought I might visit my aunt,' he said, carefully adjusting a salver so that it was perfectly aligned with the edge of the table. 'I fear I'm making up a fourth for bridge.'

'Oh, crikey,' I said. 'Is she a fearsome player?'

'Only moderately terrifying, sir,' said Beauregard. 'But she can be quite demanding in a conversational sense. She likes to be kept informed and sees me as a source of local news.'

'Nothing too juicy about me?' I asked with some trepidation.

'One can rely on my discretion, sir.'

After leaving the rent party, Amelia had walked me back to Lucy's flat before skipping off to wherever it is she lays her head at night. Or, in this case, the early morning, as we headed past all the boot boys, maids, cooks, lift attendants and doormen hurrying for the subway and the trams downtown. I let myself in and climbed into bed beside Lucy, who rolled over, complaining about Fletcher Henderson not hiring Zutty Singleton, and continued snoring. I put my arms around him and let the scent of his hair lull me to sleep.

Breakfast, whatever time we have it, is often hit-and-miss at Lucy's. So it was over a boiled egg and toast that we discussed what we planned to do that evening. Or rather, what we planned not to do. Which was to get involved with Nightingale's madcap schemes.

Before I left I made a point of laying out the correct shirt and shoes to go with Lucy's evening dress because these matters cannot, with any confidence, be left to the man himself. If it had been up to me I would have stayed happily at home with Lucy but, whatever else, I was still Nightingale's host, and so I set off downtown.

Nightingale sat down for our light lunch in the same plus-fours, boots and gaiters that he'd worn on his previous jaunt out to Long Island. A leather golf bag was propped up by the umbrella stand.

'Looking to get a round in?' I asked.

'A golf bag is a very useful shape for this sort of op,' he said. 'Which reminds me.' He reached into his jacket and withdrew an envelope, which he passed to me. It was addressed to a David Mellenby, care of the Folly on Russell Square, London.

'If I don't make it back, I'd like you to return my trunk to the Folly and send this separately,' he said. 'The old sticks will probably want a report, but I leave it to you to decide what to reveal.'

'Thomas—' I started, but he cut me off.

'Lucien is quite correct,' he said. 'I had no right to

drag you into this affair. You must forgive me, Gussie. I did not realise how much you had to lose.'

I'm sure you can imagine that I felt downright rotten for the whole duration of my bath. But shaving the old pins and chest required all my concentration, so by the time I was plucking my eyebrows I'd recovered my poise. Then it was just a question of applying the old vanishing *crème pour le visage* and I was ready for the dress.

I wore my topper and tails in the cab to Lucy's; it seemed appropriate, and if I chose to carry my heavier cane, then that was only prudence. On the way I sat upright and alert like a small boy being taken for a Christmas treat, a constant flutter of excitement in my chest.

I'd had the dress on before – Madame Zaza had to fit it and Lucy had to have his own private first-night view – but none of that is the same as when you wear it for the first time, as it were, in anger. The feel of the chiffon pressing the silk of your shift against your back and your thighs . . . The stockings tight as armour as you roll them up your legs . . . And then the shoes. Slipping them on and standing in front of the mirror. Taller, stretched out and suddenly, fabulously, being totally inside yourself in a way you never truly are at any other time.

'Can I come in yet?' called Lucy from the hall.

'Not yet,' I said, because I wanted to be perfect.

I took my time putting on my face. I know women and men who can slap on their makeup in under a minute, but I don't have their daily practice. I could practically feel Lucy's impatience radiating through the door like a *vestigium* as I finished up. When I was ready, I stood facing the door, adjusted my garter and struck a pose.

'Come in,' I called, and the door flew open and Lucy ran in.

And then stopped. And stared.

I have, as readers of my memoirs will know, had a busy life in many ways. I've travelled far and wide, often under protest, and sampled the delights of at least three continents – four, if you count Australia. But no sybaritic pleasure, no drink, no food, no wide magnificent vista can top seeing yourself reflected the way you want to be reflected in your lover's eyes.

'Well, I do declare, Augusta,' said Lucy in an exaggerated southern accent. 'If you ain't the prettiest belle of the ball.' He passed me my blue sequined half-mask and I settled it into place.

There were bigger drag balls in New York. At the start of the month, Lucy and I had shaken a fine leg at the Hamilton Lodge Ball at the Rockland Palace, where I realised – much to my chagrin – that my spiffy evening dress with its round neckline and straight hem wasn't going to cut the mustard.

You know, it's an odd thing. But until that evening I'd never thought of myself as a competitive chap. I knew plenty of them from school and university – Nightingale being a prime example of the type. Chaps who couldn't attend a three-legged race at a village fête without being desperate to win. But beyond some light betting at Goodwood and the like, I'd never allowed myself to become exercised – if that's the right word.

But no longer. Harry Walter, winner of the Hamilton Lodge masquerade, had worn an asymmetrical hemline and heels. Now I did, too, and as we swept up the red carpet in front of the Roxy Ballroom, I walked with all the confidence of a man who'd practised wearing them every day for two weeks. Flashbulbs popped and their light followed me and Lucy as if we were royalty. Better . . . as if we were Hollywood movie stars arriving at a première.

The ballroom proper was a big rectangular box with a stage at one end, a dance floor in the middle, with tables all around. Above them on a kind of balcony were the private boxes where what Lucy called the downtown gawpers gathered to enjoy the show.

'They think they're above us,' Lucy said when he saw me glancing up. 'But we're the ones down here putting on the ritz.'

The orchestra at the back of the stage was playing 'Everybody Loves My Baby' as we headed for the tables.

'Oh, my,' said a figure surging through the crowd. 'Don't you look pretty? Both of you.'

It was Amelia, or perhaps Cocoa, or perhaps somebody new. The young woman had shaved her head down to a mere shadow, the better to seat her top hat at a jaunty angle. Her mask was black velvet with black glass beads stitched to give her eyes the mischievous slant of a feline. To match mask and topper, she wore a black velvet tailcoat with matching trousers, but instead of a dress shirt, a top of some silver-blue material that was so translucent that she might as well have left it off entirely for all the modesty it provided. I couldn't take my eyes off it.

'You must tell me where you got that shirt,' I said.

'He's so single-minded,' she said to Lucy.

'And who are you today?' asked Lucy.

Amelia gave a gay laugh and, slipping between us, took our arms and led us towards a table.

'You might as well call me Cocoa,' she said. 'I'm always Cocoa on the inside.'

Cocoa had certainly got us an excellent table, not too close to the band, but right up against the dance floor and strategically placed with regards to the bar so that a steady stream of waiters passed by. Cocoa accosted one as soon as we were seated, and soon we were drinking sidecars and watching the crowd.

'Aunt A'Lelia sends her love,' said Cocoa. 'And trusts that you will emerge triumphant.'

The band broke into 'Shim Sham Shimmy' and as one the whole crowd hit the dance floor. Lucy took my hand and we jumped up to join them.

The rules of the ball were simple: if you came as a lady then you could only dance with a gentlemen, and vice versa. Where Cocoa fitted into this schema it was impossible to say, and she cheerfully danced with both me and Lucy, and with a very short white man in a bustle and a ruff. And so the night continued, with breaks for cocktails, gossip and sizing up the competition. I tried to pace myself, since the competition parade, into which I was entered, would commence at 10.30 and it wouldn't do for me to appear flushed and sweaty. I don't think men truly appreciate the effort that goes into staying beautiful. It's practically a full-time job. Certainly Lucy's evening jacket was already taking on its customary rumpled appearance when I recaptured him at the start of 'Squeeze Me'.

It was midway through that number when *she* made her presence felt. Lucy stumbled, which is not too surprising an occurrence. I tripped and I heard Cocoa swear as her partner, who looked like she bent iron bars in half for a living, stepped on her foot. The sensation passed through the dance floor – a hungry, miserable, angry feeling, gnawing like a rat at our happiness.

I looked around and spotted her, a tall, thin figure in unfashionably long white taffeta and matching veil. She moved slowly across the floor, stepping and twirling to a different, sadder rhythm. Lloyd Beaumont, the pianist at the Alexandra, had said she couldn't dance, but it was obvious to me that she could, only she was stepping to a tune nobody else could hear.

'Damn,' I heard Cocoa say.

'Is that her?' asked Lucy.

'Let's go back to the table,' I said.

Now, I have to say that the only reason I didn't immediately hide under said table was the iron will of the Berrycloth-Youngs, and the fact that such an action could seriously disarrange my dress. As I said previously, beauty does not come without sacrifice.

We did indulge in a round of white ladies – which is essentially a sidecar, only made with bathtub gin – that had a dashed fine kick and helped soothe my nerves.

Thankfully, it was only a matter of time before the cloud of Maurelle's presence passed from the face of the sun, and light and laughter were quickly restored.

I think Lucy, Cocoa and I, not to mention the Roxy Ballroom itself, might even have survived the evening unscathed if it hadn't been for a sudden call of nature. Now that the hour approached, the prospect of parading, on my own, in front of the assembled crowd had made me unaccountably nervous, and so I went in search of a suitable venue to relieve myself. Both the Gentlemen's and the Ladies' on the ground floor were filled to bursting, but I knew there were additional facilities on the floor above. Up the stairs there were two long hallways allowing access to the boxes, where even now the gawpers were ogling the show from above like visitors to Bedlam. Emerging from the stairwell, I spied – much to my relief – a Ladies' powder room across the hall, and had just reached it when the queerest couple came running around the far corner.

One I recognised immediately as Mr. Clydesdale, aka the Horse; the other was a small child of perhaps five whom he was holding above his head as he ran. He held her by the waist as she stretched horizontally, with arms flung out as if flying. Her skin was, as foreshadowed, the colour of old ivory, and her hair, escaping from tight braids, was a shocking platinum blonde. Her eyes were hidden by dainty child-sized aviator's goggles with smoked lenses, and her mouth was open in a happy scream.

This could only be Maurelle's child, and I flattened myself against the wall in a most unladylike manner.

As the Horse thundered past, the girl turned her head to look at me.

'Stop, stop, stop,' she yelled down at her steed, who obediently skidded to a halt.

I didn't wait to watch her dismount. Instead, I pushed my way into the powder room, waved at the attendant, found an empty stall and locked myself in. For a moment I thought I might have escaped, but then I heard the hallway door creak open and Mr. Clydesdale's high-pitched, musical voice remonstrating with his charge.

'You can't come in here,' I heard the child say. 'It's for ladies only.'

Then the door closing and small footsteps slapping on the tiled floor.

The attendant asked whether the child needed help, but was politely rebuffed.

The footsteps stopped outside my stall.

'Hello,' said the child, and her voice had lost the brashness with which she had addressed Mr. Clydesdale or even the polite firmness she had used on the attendant. This voice was timid but determined. 'Hello. My name is Oriande. What's yours?'

I looked around wildly for escape, but while the stall was equipped with a window for ventilation, it was far too small for me to wriggle out of.

'You smell funny,' said Oriande. 'Are you a fairy? My mama is a fairy.'

According to my watch, I had at least fifteen minutes before the parade. All I had to do was stay quiet and wait for the child to lose interest and wander off.

'My mama says that one day we'll be rescued,' said Oriande in a sad little voice. 'But you know what? I think she's just making things up. Do *you* think we'll be rescued?'

I thought that her rescuer was probably even now breaking into a big house far away on Long Island. Which begged the question – did she really need rescuing? It was then that I made my fatal mistake . . . but it's true that I've always been led astray by my soft heart.

'Do you need rescuing, dear?' I asked, taking care to pitch my voice as high as I could without cracking.

'Mama isn't happy,' said Oriande. 'She cries when she thinks I can't hear her, and she says she wishes she could go across the sea to live in the forest again. She says that she has sent ever so many messages that somebody is bound to come rescue us.'

'Good-oh,' I said.

'Are you sure it's not you?' she asked.

'I'm sorry,' I said.

'It's OK,' said Oriande in a small voice, and I heard her disconsolate steps.

Now, I know what you're thinking: 'Gussie, this is really too much. What kind of a person are you that you refuse to help a little girl in her hour of need? The shame of it. What would your parents say? What would your headmaster have said if he could see you now?'

They'd demand to know why I was wearing a dress and having carnal relations with a coloured American chappie. That's what they would have said. Although, no doubt once they'd worked their way through that list of sins, they'd be pretty damned miffed with me for not immediately rising to the occasion.

I checked the time. I had ten minutes before the parade.

It was then I conceived a corker of a plan. Which just goes to show that even the limited brain of Augustus Berrycloth-Young is, when push comes to shove, capable of great things.

If all that was stopping Maurelle from escaping on her own was the fact that her child was held hostage, then should I spirit away the child, her mother would be perfectly capable of taking matters into her own hands. Nightingale needn't be involved, except perhaps to provide passage back to Blighty and suffer the opprobrium of the old sticks at the Folly.

After all, what was the point of wearing a mask to a masquerade if you couldn't hide behind it?

I left the sanctuary of my stall and, pausing only to tip the attendant, slipped out into the hallway. Oriande and her goonish nanny were nowhere to be seen, but I could hear her yelling cheerfully from around the corner. I headed after them and, as I did, a tall figure in a beautiful crimson dress, with matching shawl and mask, emerged from one of the boxes.

Normally I would have stopped to inquire where they had obtained their dress, but time was pressing, so I nodded politely and hurried past as fast I could in my heels. I turned the corner onto the long balcony that ran above the orchestra, just in time to come face to face with Oriande as she reluctantly dismounted from the Horse.

'Hello,' I said, holding out my hand. 'Would you like to be in a parade?'

'Yes, please,' said Oriande, seizing my hand.

The Horse stepped forward to remonstrate, but I adopted the tone and manner of my dear old mater, who never would take any interference from anyone. In fact, she once upbraided a High Court judge in his own court while she was giving evidence.

'You don't mind me borrowing your darling child?' I said. 'Just for a few minutes, I promise. I just know if she parades with me, I shall win for sure.' I checked my watch. 'Look at the time. I'll have her right back, I promise.'

I don't know whether Mr. Clydesdale was bamboozled by my manner, or had been instructed not to make waves, but the poor chap halted and looked flustered. I was about to take advantage and sweep off when a small sound caused my blood to freeze in my veins.

And the sound of a revolver being cocked is a very small sound in the scheme of things. The sort of small noise one might overlook, what with the girl's happy shrieks and the muffled jazz floating up from the ballroom.

But not when it occurs a scant few inches behind one's head.

'Ah,' said a familiar voice. 'If it isn't *Miss* Bertram Wilberforce, acclaimed London musicologist and fag about town. Although I have to say you do look rather swell as a girl.'

11

I t was Mr. Charles Jaeger – and I was quite pleased that he was a talkative style of cove, given the alternatives.

'And the dress is splendid,' he said. 'Where's your friend?'

Nobody likes to be in mortal peril – except perhaps Thomas Nightingale – not least because the old bean has a tendency to work in a less than satisfactory manner. Which probably explains why my next words were, 'Which one?'

'Not the n—r,' he said. 'The Englishman.'

'I wish I knew,' I said.

The Horse had approached Oriande and put both meaty paws on her shoulders. The little girl squeezed my hand.

'Let go of the child,' said Mr. Jaeger, and added, 'Now, if you will,' when I hesitated.

I let go and the Horse drew Oriande away. She looked up at me with a stricken expression.

'Don't worry,' I said. 'Everything will turn out just spiffy, you'll see.'

'That's the spirit, Miss Wilberforce,' said Mr. Jaeger.

'Or should I call you Augustus Berrycloth-Young?' He rattled off my address – which, had my blood not already been the temperature of the sort of water one associates with icebergs and penguins, would have chilled it further.

Down in the ballroom I heard the orchestra's brass section break into an up-tempo fanfare. The parade had begun, all my hard work had been wasted and – worse – by the time the next ball came around, my wonderful dress would be out of date.

For some reason, this didn't seem to matter.

Mr. Jaeger told the Horse to take the girl to 'the others'.

'And then get on the horn to Bracknel and tell him to get going straight away,' he said. 'The chimes of midnight will just have to sound early this evening.'

The Horse started dragging Oriande away.

'Now . . .' started Mr. Jaeger. And if I had to guess, based on my extensive reading, he was about to continue, 'what are we going to do with you?' But little Oriande had her own plans. She fetched the Horse such a kick on the shins that the big man shouted and let go of her arm. Before he could grab it again, she darted forward towards me.

I felt I should do something appropriately heroic at that point, but before I could formulate a plan I felt a shock to the back of my head and I stumbled forward on to my knees. There was no pain, but darkness was closing around my vision and I found it impossible to do more than stop myself toppling further.

I've been shot, I thought, and I haven't even done anything heroic.

I felt Oriande throw her arms around my neck, and that's when the pain and a need to vomit nearly overwhelmed me. I had the rummiest thought that the pain meant I probably wasn't dead. But what would I know? I've never been shot before.

'You promised,' Oriande hissed in my ear, sounding annoyed. Which I thought was extremely unfair.

A very long way away, Mr. Jaeger was giving instructions to the Horse.

'Get Pat and Owlsey up here,' he said. 'I'll take care of these two, since that seems beyond your talents.'

I didn't like the sound of being taken care of, so I summoned up my courage and put my hand to the back of my head. It was tender and hurt like the blazes, but was gloriously free of any bullet holes. I felt suddenly a great deal more chipper – I suppose not being shot can do that. But unfortunately Mr. Jaeger proved himself a bit of a mind-reader.

'Stay down, you stupid faggot,' he snarled. 'Or I'll shoot you for sure.'

There was still a dire throbbing at the back of my head, but the urge to revisit my supper had waned. I shifted my position – slowly, so as not to alarm the maniac with a gun – so that I could see said maniac.

And the gun, of course, which was still distressingly aimed in my general direction.

Oriande tightened her grip on me, her face puckered into an expression of determination.

'What the f—k is going on out here?' said someone. 'Charles, is that you?'

The gawpers must have left their boxes and were

loudly demanding to know what was happening. I subsequently heard that both the Rockefellers and Langston Hughes were there that night but, being on my knees, I was not in a position to confirm this. I did feel Maurelle before I saw her, the rage pouring off her like heat from an open oven.

Jaeger grabbed Oriande and put her between him and her mother. He didn't do anything so gauche as to aim the revolver at the girl, but the threat was implied.

'Maurelle,' said Jaeger. 'Get rid of these people.'

She hesitated, rigid with indecision, before turning to hiss at the crowd of swells who had begun to fill the balcony. I felt it myself . . . what we learned magical types call the *seducere* or the glamour. The assembled gawpers turned and shuffled off back towards their boxes, which was pretty dashed impressive for a single fae. It was then that the omnibus of reason made a sudden reappearance and collided with the bean of Berrycloth-Young. Jaeger wasn't keeping Maurelle for her skill with enchanting musical instruments. It was her glamour that Jaeger sought to utilise. How many deals had she tipped in his favour? How many rivals had been compelled into making mistakes?

I was so taken with my own cleverness that it took me a moment to notice that one of the gawpers had defied the glamour and stayed where they were. It was the figure in the crimson dress, taking a most unfeminine stance with hands on hips and shoulders thrown back. Despite the scarlet mask and headdress, I suddenly had no doubt as to who this was.

'Mr. Jaeger,' said Nightingale. 'This has all gone far enough. I suggest you release Maurelle and the girl into my care, and we can all walk away from this with the minimum of unpleasantness.'

'Well, my ancestors fought at Valley Forge,' said Mr. Jaeger. 'So no dice.'

Nightingale took a step forward, but before he could act further, Jaeger seized Oriande around the waist and called upon Maurelle to 'Kill that man.' Without hesitating, and rather alarmingly, Maurelle threw herself at Nightingale, who raised his hand and conjured an invisible shield to fend her off.

'Gussie,' he shouted. 'Grab the girl.'

One thing I'll say for Mr. Jaeger: he was not slow on the uptake. He immediately took another swing at me with the butt of the revolver, but I was already rolling out of the way. I kicked out wildly and must have caught him with the narrow heel of my shoe, because he cursed and hopped back. I jumped up and confronted him, readying my own shield spell in case he tried to shoot me. Behind me I could hear wood splintering as Maurelle and Nightingale biffed it out, but I didn't dare look round because Jaeger fired once, twice, three times. The shield took two shots, but the third whiffled past my head in a most unpleasant fashion.

Now I'd nerved myself up to smack Jaeger in the head with an *impello palma* but, before I could, the worryingly equine Mr. Clydesdale came running up behind him, backed by a pair of goons I recognised from our boat trip. All carried pistols and didn't hesitate for a moment when Jaeger told them to open fire.

Since discretion is the better part of valour, I vaulted over the balcony and dropped into the ballroom below. As I fell, I could see that the hopeful contestants, oblivious to the shooting going on above their heads, were lined up on the stage awaiting the signal to parade around the edge of the dance floor.

I'm going to make the contest after all, I thought as the stage rushed up to meet me.

No wizard has figured out a way to fly yet, but there are a couple of spells a chap might use *in extremis* to break his fall. *Extremis* like vaulting a banister twenty feet above the stage in the Roxy. It's the sort of thing a chap might use when escaping out of the private rooms of a public house when an uncharitable landlord has called the rozzers over a minor disagreement with regards to the bill. As a result, it is one of the few spells I can do in a hurry while squiffy. It sort of thickens the air near the ground, so that it slows one's fall just prior to impact. Timing is crucial or you break a shin bone – or worse. Mine was a bit off, and I staggered on landing. I heard a crack and a leg went out from under me. I'd broken a heel, but I didn't get a chance to mourn because the goons on the balcony opened fire.

The line-up of hopeful queens dissolved into panic, and I threw a scatter of fireballs up at the trigger men. They were slow-moving, noisy things, the sort you use for japes on Guy Fawkes Night, but they had the desired effect of causing the goons to stop shooting and scatter.

It may also just be possible that they are what set the Roxy Ballroom on fire that night, but we will never know for sure.

I limped back into the shelter of the balcony over-hang and watched the crowd stampeding for the exit. Presumably Jaeger would be doing the same and taking Oriande with him. He'd have a car nearby. So, to stop him I'd have to escape the Roxy and cut him off before he could reach it.

Nightingale was counting on me to recover the girl, and now I was going to be forced to do it in stockinged feet. But not alone, because Lucy and Cocoa quickly joined me.

'We need to get out,' I said.

'There's bulls blocking the side doors,' said Cocoa. 'It's a raid.'

So we joined the perfumed herd making for the main entrance, but unfortunately that was also replete with members of the local constabulary. I didn't care, because my blood was up. And when the blood of the Berrycloth-Youngs is up, it's . . . Well, it's jolly well up is all I am saying.

When I spotted the same bejowled specimen of corrupt policing as had terrorised us in Lucy's flat, I decided that luck had been, if not a lady, then a magnificent queen tonight. Sergeant Bracknel was standing between the crowd and the exit, with his hands on his hips and a sneer on his lips.

'Everybody can f—king stay where they are,' he shouted, spittle flying from his lips. 'You all know the drill by now – I want those purses turned out, and woe betide any of you faggots who tries to cheat me.'

Now some of these 'faggots' I knew to be longshore-men who worked the docks, and the type of chaps who would gladly punch a policeman regardless of what it might do to their manicure. The longshoreman's manicure, not the police officer's, I mean. But backing up this despicable sergeant was a line of policemen, brandishing their truncheons and looking very much like they relished the idea of using them.

'There's no point trying to fight them,' Lucy had said. 'They always get their licks in.'

I may not be the greatest practitioner to have graced the playing fields of Casterbrook, I may have chosen to squander my talents on pranks and japes, and I, most definitely, am not in the weight class of Nightingale . . .

But I am a keeper of the secret flame, a sayer of the three sacred oaths, and a man who carries a staff of power.

Except when it clashed with that evening's outfit.

But, metaphorically speaking, I carry it with me wherever I go.

First I seized the officers' truncheons and belaboured them around their faces. While they staggered under that onslaught, I snapped their belts so that their deeply unattractive blue wool trousers fell around their knees. I probably didn't need to flourish my hand to grab hold of the soles of the clodhopping boots and yank their owners off their feet.

But I always say, if you can't put a bit of showmanship into your magic, what's the bally point?

The crowd had fallen into a sudden silence, and this had obviously intimated to Sergeant Bracknel that things were going awry. He turned to goggle at his fallen men, who were even then writhing around on the floor in a pleasing mixture of pain and embarrassment.

I used that interlude to work my way to the front of the crowd, because what I was about to attempt needed a bit of finesse, some daring and a great deal of concentration. Because tonight at the Spring Masquerade, Sergeant Unpleasant of the New York Police Department was about to be well and truly *Crockered*.

Crocker was one of those bright boys who are given a scholarship so that they may suffer the delights of boarding school life. He was before my time, but a bit of a legend, and the legend was that his family were in the rag trade in Manchester and that the precocious Crocker had sought to adapt magic to assist his parents' profession. The result was a spell, designed to pull garments apart at the seams, that has been passed down by generations of merry-hearted pranksters. No doubt Nightingale knows it, but I doubt the old sticks of the Folly council do.

One peculiarity of the Crocker Process, as it is known to those in the know, is that it only works on clothes that are being worn at the time. Something to do with the topographical conformity with the subject's morphological field, but I admit I may have been asleep for most of that class.

It's a complicated spell – fifth or seventh order, depending on how you count your *inflectes* – but I've always been rather good at it. And during my university days it provided me with a great deal of happiness. I've also had it cast on me, so I happened to know for a fact that the victim of the spell is aware, for just a moment, of the sense of thousands of little fingers sliding along their bare skin. That part is not nearly as much fun as it sounds, although some – more adventurous – chaps I know swear by it as a warm-up, so to speak, before intimacy.

Bracknel gave a startled squawk as his uniform was ripped from his body, leaving him standing with bare arms and legs akimbo. I was disappointed to note that he still favoured a woollen all-in-one union suit, but at least had the decency to own a proper pair of sock gaiters.

He looked first at his own state of undress, then at the crowd staring back. It was hard to say who was more shocked, and the impasse might have endured had not the distinctive sound of gunshots sounded from somewhere up in the ballroom.

The crowd surged forward, and that was the last I ever saw of Sergeant Bracknel, although Lucy assured me he survived relatively unscathed and went to live with a maiden aunt in Jersey City. Which, in Cocoa's opinion, was a fate worse than death. I was amazed to hear he'd survived, because we only made it out to the street by allowing ourselves to be carried along in the tide of red velvet, pink taffeta, and a particularly nice mink stole I was tempted to snatch as I was swept past.

Out on Seventh Avenue, it had started to rain. The masquerade crowd was legging it and mingling with the inevitable crowd of local sightseers – there being nothing a Harlem crowd loves more than a free show. A line of black police cars were being guarded by a couple of officers who had drawn their revolvers and were looking around for someone to shoot.

I heard a childish scream of rage and, looking over the heads of the milling crowd, I spotted Jaeger carrying Oriande across the avenue. Ahead of him was parked a bright yellow Rickenbacker two-seater, with the large shape of Mr. Clydesdale waiting nervously beside it.

Seventh Avenue is the widest in Harlem, and I've met enough chappies who fought in the war to feel a bit queasy when running across open ground against armed opponents. Something I've done surprisingly often in my career, in spite of my strenuous efforts to avoid armed opponents, open ground, or indeed serious exertion of any kind.

Thus it was I had my shield up when Mr. Clydesdale opened fire. What with the ruination of my dress, my missed opportunity to be declared Queen of the Spring Ball and my broken heel, I was not minded to be kind to Mr. Clydesdale. And so, once I had separated him from his pistol, I threw him into the basement area of a nearby speakeasy.

Unfortunately, this gave Jaeger time to bundle Oriande into the two-seater and drive off like Mr. Toad, in a furious roar and screech of tyres.

'Blast,' I said.

Nightingale arrived to stand beside me. His feathered headdress was missing but, like me, he'd kept the mask and most of his dress.

'Was that Jaeger?' he asked.

'It was.'

'Blast,' he said.

I was about to say that we needed our own wheels when Lucy pulled up in a black Ford with Cocoa standing on the running board. I was about to ask where he'd obtained the car when a fusillade of shots peppered it from behind. I looked and saw half a dozen angry policemen running towards us and waving their pistols in a most animated fashion.

'Is this a police car?' I asked Lucy.

'It was the only one with the engine running,' he said.

'Get in,' said Nightingale.

'Get going,' said Cocoa. 'I'll take care of the cops.'

'I say—' started Nightingale, but before he could say more, Lucy put his foot down. I looked back and saw Cocoa walking jauntily back towards the line of police, swinging a cane. My cane, I realised, and wondered whether she knew how to use its hidden potential. I never got a chance to see, because at that moment Lucy swung us right into a cross-street and I lost sight of her.

I asked Nightingale what had happened to Maurelle.

'Fortunately, I managed to interpose a number of Jaeger's men between us and, while she was distracted, made my escape.' He leaned out of the car to check our rear. 'But I doubt she will be far behind us.'

I've heard New York called 'the city that never sleeps' and, certainly unlike London, the traffic barely falters until the early hours. If anything, with fewer pedestrians everyone drives faster. Especially the cabbies. Certainly Lucy did so, particularly when Nightingale found the switch that activated the siren.

It was great fun to be roaring along in the back seat of

a flivver and being on the wrong side, as it were, of that whooping siren.

Lucy shouted something. I leaned forward to hear him.

'He's nowhere to be seen,' said Lucy.

'He'll be heading for Long Island,' said Nightingale. 'Make for the Queensboro Bridge.'

'What if he takes his boat?' I asked.

'Once I realised no one was at the house,' said Nightingale, 'I took the liberty of sinking it on my return to the city. We know where he's going. We just need to catch up before he gets there.'

'He's in a Rickenbacker,' I said. 'And this is a Ford.'

'Good point,' said Nightingale.

At that moment, racing down the tunnel formed by the houses and the elevated train track above our heads, the streetlamps and passing cars thwapping past like the horn blares of 'Daybreak Express', even if back then Duke Ellington had not yet conceived that particular gem, and the shrill of the siren echoing back off the buildings like Cootie Williams' shrieking solo, watching the quick motions of Lucy's head as he guided our passage with total concentration . . .

For that moment, I thought I might understand just what it was like to be Thomas Nightingale.

Lucy swerved onto the roadway up to the Queensboro Bridge, throwing me painfully against the door and reminding me that I was not the redoubtable Nightingale, but rather good old Gussie Berrycloth-Young, and I liked nightclubs and jazz, cups of coffee in the morning, and long slow evenings with Lucy.

As we entered the lower deck of the bridge, Nightingale cut the siren.

'A bridge is a psychological break,' he said, which frankly mystified me. 'With luck, Mr. Jaeger will believe himself to be free of pursuit and slow his pace. We may be able to catch up.'

The borough of Queens is much like Manhattan or the Bronx – townhouses, tenements, mansions and elevated railways. It was less busy than Manhattan and Lucy picked up the pace as best as the old Ford could manage.

There are, Lucy explained, half a dozen different routes through Queens, but if you're heading for Manhasset, then once you were past the great burning reek of Flushing, it was the road they, confusingly, named Broadway.

And dashed if Nightingale hadn't been right, because on a straight stretch just past Little Neck we caught sight of a flash of the yellow two-seater caught in the headlamps of an overtaking car.

Jaeger may have been dawdling by the standards of the Rickenbacker, but our poor flivver was growling and snarling just to close the gap.

'Damn it,' shouted Nightingale. 'He's almost home.'

I realised that I recognised the lane we were speeding down. It was the same one in which we had stumbled on Cocoa sleeping in a car. Jaeger's estate could only be half a mile further up. Nightingale tensed, and I guessed he was about to risk clipping the fleeing car's rear wheel. I was fearfully anxious, and looked to see what I could do. Which meant I was staring straight at Oriande when she made her move.

The car swerved, and Jaeger tried to stop as she jumped to her feet and, throwing her arms around his head, pulled backwards. It's just possible that she was trying to break his neck, but we'll never know.

The rummy thing is that my memory of what happened next is in pieces: flashes of images and bursts of noise, all scattered out of order. So sometimes looking back I hear the crunching sound of our flivver striking the back of Jaeger's car before I see said flivver swerving and flopping over on its side. Lucy is shouting; Nightingale hisses an expletive over and over again.

And then there is the taste of grass and the smell of burning rubber and the stars above.

Then suddenly the whole dashed experience crashes back down, and I find I am lying on my back on the grassy verge, staring up at the sky.

'Gussie,' shouts Nightingale. 'I need a werelight. Now, dammit!'

I sat up and conjured a werelight with almost no thought at all. Well, he was a prefect when I was a bug. And while I didn't fag for him directly, I'd been collared by him for jobs often enough to jump to it on command.

Ahead, illuminated by my conjuration, was Jaeger's Rickenbacker, still on its side. Beside me was our stolen flivver, its bonnet crumpled and front wheels splayed flat. I looked around wildly for Lucy and sighed relief when he turned out to be standing beside me.

'Are you OK?' he asked, and helped me to my feet.

'Where's the girl?' I asked.

'Here,' called Nightingale, emerging from behind the

two-seater with Oriande in his arms. When she saw us, she squirmed out of his grasp and ran towards us.

'I went up in the air,' she said brightly.

'Did you?' I said, and picked her up. She was a heavy little thing.

'What happened to Jaeger?' asked Lucy.

Nightingale made a casual gesture with his left hand and, with a groan, the two-seater righted itself back on to its wheels, which promptly collapsed. Jaeger was still in the front seat and looking, unfortunately, not very much worse for wear. He turned his head and gave us a baleful look. His mouth worked as if he wanted to say something, but he couldn't think of anything terrible enough to curse us with. He clawed at the side door, which resisted until finally he swivelled in his seat and kicked it open.

Charles Jaeger came out of his car like a Fury bent on terrible retribution but, before either Nightingale or I could act, Lucy shot him twice, in the chest, with his revolver.

The man looked positively nonplussed by the development, but then his eyes rolled up and he fell on his face.

Lucien turned to face us and returned his revolver to his pocket.

'My apologies, gentlemen, but if you take a moment to consider the facts, you'll see that was the only way,' he said. 'A rich white man like that would not take an affront to his power lightly. He owned the police, the politicians and the gangsters. Gussie and I would not have survived for very long.'

I expected Nightingale to make at least a token protest, but instead he shrugged.

'Help me get him back in the car,' he said.

Since I was holding Oriande, I was spared the gruesome task of levering Jaeger's body back into the two-seater. Oriande said nothing. Outraged, shocked, stunned? I couldn't tell.

'I think even the local sheriff will notice he's been shot in the chest,' said Lucy as we walked away from the crash.

'This will not be a problem,' said Nightingale, and clicked his fingers.

I sensed the clockwork catch of his magic and behind us the car exploded. I felt the heat of it on my back and hurried on.

'I see,' said Lucy looking back. 'That's a neat trick.'

'A useful one, certainly,' said Nightingale.

'Much as I love a stroll in the moonlight,' I said, 'I feel the sight of us in a state of *déshabillé* may provoke comment.'

'In Queens?' said Lucy. 'They'll just think you're a local.'

'So, how did you get that dress?' I asked Nightingale.

'It wasn't easy,' he said.

I might have pressed for more, but at that moment we were illuminated by the headlights of an oncoming sedan, which pulled up beside us. Oriande shrieked and wriggled out of my arms. There was an answering cry and Maurelle squirmed out of the side window like an eel and swept up her daughter in her arms.

While they spun in a little happy dance, the sedan's

driver's door opened to reveal Cocoa wearing a police-man's tunic and a grin.

'Hey, do you ladies need a lift?' she said.

C ocoa drove us back to my flat, which Nightingale
pointed out was both larger than Lucy's and more
defensible. To my astonishment, Beauregard was waiting up for us when we returned, and showed no surprise at the inclusion of Maurelle and her daughter in
our party. Given recent events, I was loath to let Lucy
out of my sight, a policy with which Nightingale, to my
continued astonishment, concurred.

'The police know his address,' he said. 'Best that he
stays here until the situation is clarified.'

Since Maurelle and Oriande were in the guest room,
Beauregard made up the sofa for Nightingale and sug-
gested that Lucy should share my bed, which caused
Lucy to choke on his nightcap.

'*In extremis,*' said Beauregard, 'there's nothing un-
toward about good friends sharing.'

Cocoa saw us settled and then departed for a party in
the village.

'The night is young,' she said.

'Yes it is,' said Lucy as we retired.

The morning was also young when Lucy and I were

awoken by Oriande jumping up and down on my bed.

'I saw an airplane,' she said.

'How nice,' said Lucy, and pulled the covers over his head.

I sat up and she stood in front of me, face to face, as if defying me to react.

Her eyes were an extraordinarily beautiful hazel colour flecked with gold and red and, indeed, slotted just like a goat's. When the sunlight struck her face, she frowned and shaded her eyes with her hand.

'Do you have an airplane?' she asked.

I admitted that I did not, which seemed to disappoint her.

'Why not?' she demanded.

I vouchsafed that it had never occurred to me to buy an aeroplane, which Oriande seemed to find an extraordinary oversight on my part.

Beauregard wafted in with coffee on a tray and, with barely a glance at Lucy's recumbent form, turned to Oriande and held out her smoked glass goggles.

'I believe the young lady mislaid these,' he said.

Oriande slipped them on and, distracted by whatever thought processes drive the actions of small children, jumped off the bed and scuttled out.

'I'm afraid breakfast this morning will be without bacon, liver or kidneys,' said Beauregard.

This was a blow. I'd been counting on a proper breakfast.

'The young lady's mother,' explained Beauregard, 'became somewhat peckish during the night and seized upon the same for a midnight feast. Fortunately, she did not attempt to operate the range, or the outcome could have been a great deal more severe.'

'What? She ate them raw?'

'I believe so, sir.'

'All of them?' I asked, since I knew Beauregard liked to keep the larder well stocked.

'The lady's appetite is certainly prodigious.'

'I know it's Sunday, but I suggest we order in fresh supplies *tout suite.*'

'A wise precaution,' said Beauregard.

Later that morning Cocoa arrived, trailed by half a dozen young coloured boys carrying steamer trunks and freshly wrapped parcels.

'Gifts from the Queen of Joy,' said Cocoa.

Said gifts, I couldn't help notice, consisting mostly of all the clothes, toiletries and amusements that a mother and daughter might need on a steamer heading for Europe. There was much frenetic activity as Cocoa, Oriande and Maurelle tried on all the clothes. Lucy slept through the whole thing, but Nightingale and I took ourselves down to the shipping office to book passage for three on the SS *De Grasse.*

The clerk protested that all the first-class accommodation had been booked, but I bribed him by promising to obtain tickets for *The Girl Friend* at the Vanderbilt, plus a hefty wad of cabbage, as they say here. Nightingale was suitably grateful and promised to wire me the money once he was in London.

As we strolled back to Washington Square I extolled my theory, formulated *in extremis*, I might add, that

Charles Jaeger had been using Maurelle's glamour to buy influence and power.

'Lucien did say that he harboured political ambitions,' I said.

'He would have been stopped,' said Nightingale. 'The Americans aren't any keener on that sort of thing than we are.'

'I've seen nothing official since I arrived here,' I said.

'You might want to keep it that way,' said Nightingale. 'Assuming you stay.'

'Do you think I should?'

We stopped in the square for a moment to enjoy the green.

'I've never really understood what you might call physical love,' said Nightingale. 'But I do understand the bonds of friendship and family. You and Lucien are in love, and God knows that's precious enough to be worth fighting for. But, more importantly, worth ignoring what polite society has to say on the matter.'

I was literally struck dumb at that moment, which I think Nightingale took for incomprehension, for he grinned at me.

'Get a house somewhere, fill it full of Lucien and jazz and whatever else takes your fancy,' he said. 'I'll tell the old sticks at the Folly you're discreetly keeping an eye on the Americans.'

'And will I be keeping an eye?'

'The occasional letter, Gussie,' said Nightingale. 'So I know you're doing well.'

We strolled on while I digested this and the old bean,

obviously seeking a safer topic of conversation, advanced a notion which I put into words.

'If Maurelle was kept around to put the 'fluence on bigwigs and whatnot,' I said, 'what were all the visits to the balls and nightclubs about?'

'She may draw a form of sustenance from the excitement and the emotions,' said Nightingale. 'Perhaps she'll tell me on the voyage home.'

'And where will "home" be?'

'That's up to Maurelle,' said Nightingale. 'If she has no other plans, I know a family in Kent where mother and daughter would pass without too much comment.'

'I suppose your friend Milly—'

'Molly.'

'Your friend Molly will be pleased.'

'I expect she will bake me a cake.'

The next morning we arose early to travel down to the docks, to wave goodbye and ensure Nightingale departed safely. Cocoa met us there, presumably so she could report back to A'Lelia Walker.

'Well, he's a sinner,' said Cocoa as the liner was pulled away by tugs, gulls dipping and screaming above. 'Candy-coated.'

'Just as long as he sins on the other side of the Atlantic,' I said.

After that, we repaired to my apartment for lunch.

I had, of course, sounded out Beauregard in advance and asked if he could see his way to take up butlering as a profession. He said he would be most satisfied to act in that capacity, providing it was left to him to select the staff. If you must, I conceded, and rejoiced that the task would not fall to me.

That left only one last possible impediment, and even as I hesitated to raise it, Beauregard anticipated the very contingency.

'Will Mr. Gibbs be joining the household?' he asked.

I said he would and, tentatively, as a boy asking for more gruel in a workhouse, I inquired if this would create a difficulty.

'Not at all,' said Beauregard. 'Mr. Gibbs is a fine young man from an excellent family. His only disadvantage is his lack of sartorial flair.'

'This is true, Mr. Beauregard,' I said. 'Perhaps together we can work to remedy that.'

'Quite so, sir,' said Beauregard.

Over lunch I put the proposition to Lucy himself. He was agreeable on two conditions.

'This house will, of course, be above 110th Street?' he said.

'Naturally,' I said. 'There's bound to be a suitable property on Edgecombe or 138th.'

'And a second condition that you might not like so much.'

'Anything, dear heart,' I said, although not without the tiniest twinge of trepidation.

'You say magic is like jazz,' he said.

'And so it is,' I said.

'Good,' said Lucien. 'Because I want you to teach me.'

Historical Note

A'Lelia Walker was a real person and the story of her life and times is worth reading up on, as is that of her mother, Madame C. J. Walker, who built a business out of nothing in the teeth of personal and institutional racism and sexism. The Harlem Renaissance was equally astonishing, as was the flowering of queer culture that went alongside it. New York has always seen itself as *the* metropolis, the beating heart of the modern world, and however sceptically we view that claim now, in the 1920s it was incontrovertibly true.

I couldn't find any reliable plans for the Savoy or the Rockland Palace, so I have invented a venue for my imaginary Spring Masquerade, but I have tried to stay true to the extraordinary spirit of the times.

THE FURTHER ADVENTURES OF
THE REMARKABLE BEAUREGARD ...

GUSSIE GOES WEST
Bertram D. Argyll

'In anticipation of such an eventuality I took the liberty of engaging a stevedore this morning.'
A delightful collection of the earliest Beauregard and Gussie short stories, including *The Affair of the Goodwin Toppers*, *Enter Beauregard* and *Gussie the Bootlegger*.

BEAUREGARD PLAYS A BLINDER
Bertram D. Argyll

'I believe this is what sir might call a "sticky wicket".'
When the cast of the Broadway musical *Oh-Kay* challenge the might of the British Consulate's cricket team, the odds are so stacked against the American upstarts that not even a sporting gentleman such as Gussie is tempted to place a bet. But when he learns that a close chum has bet their fortune on an American win, Gussie must turn to his indomitable butler for help. But can even the talented Beauregard master the arcane art of cricket in less than a week?

THE CASTLE OF MISSING MEN
Bertram D. Argyll

'Ah, Gussie, I have a little problem in Memphis that I need a white man to sort out.'

Dispatched by formidable society doyen Madam Walker to Memphis to extricate an errant niece from a little 'local difficulty', our hero is about to discover just why they call that city the place where the blues come from. Caught between local mobsters, predatory bar owners, wayward musicologists and an old man who claims to be the spirit of the mighty Mississippi, this might even be beyond the extraordinary Beauregard.

INTO THE GREAT WHITE NORTH
Bertram D. Argyll

'A telegram from the Folly is never a cause for celebration and for a moment I seriously considered legging it out the parlour window. If I'd had any inkling of what was ahead I would have run all the way to Poughkeepsie, the Hudson River be damned.'

Dispatched across the 49th parallel by the old sticks at the Folly to assist the Mounties in an unusual manhunt, Gussie must brave the winter cold, hostile Quebecois and a distressing lack of the accoutrements of civilisation. And all that is before he even encounters the moose with attitude.

Acknowledgements

Writing is a time consuming business and could not be carried out without the support, encouragement and occasional stern talkings too by those that surround us. So it is with deep gratitude that I'd like to thank Anne, Sara, Genn, Clive, Stevie, my fellow writers Andrew Cartmel and James Swallow and my agent John Berlyne for their support, expertise and hard work on my behalf.

Credits

Ben Aaronovitch and Orion Fiction would like to thank everyone at Orion who worked on the publication of *The Masquerades of Spring* in the UK.

Agent
John Berlyne

Editorial
Emad Akhtar
Sarah O'Hara

Copyeditor
Steve O'Gorman

Proofreader
John Garth

Audio
Paul Stark
Alana Gaglio

Contracts

Dan Herron
Ellie Bowker
Alyx Hurst

Design
Tomás Almeida
Joanna Ridley

Editorial Management
Charlie Panayiotou
Jane Hughes
Bartley Shaw

Finance
Jasdip Nandra
Nick Gibson
Sue Baker

Marketing
Tom Noble

Javerya Iqbal
Hennah Sandhu

Production
Ruth Sharvell

Publicity
Leanne Oliver
Jenna Petts

Sales
Jen Wilson
Esther Waters
Victoria Laws
Toluwalope Ayo-Ajala
Karin Burnik
Frances Doyle
Rachael Hum
Ellie Kyrke-Smith
Sinead White
Georgina Cutler

Operations
Jo Jacobs
Dan Stevens

'Witty, well plotted, vividly written and addictively readable' *The Times*

#1 RIVERS OF LONDON:
Life takes a turn for the strange when DC Peter Grant takes a witness statement from a ghost. Transferred to the department that the police would rather not admit exists, Peter becomes the first trainee wizard on the force for fifty years.

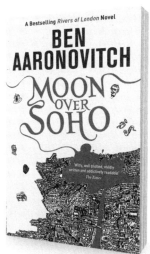

#2 MOON OVER SOHO:
A Soho jazz saxophonist seemingly falls dead of a heart attack right after finishing a gig. But Peter can still hear music around the body, and he knows this is no ordinary case. Something – or *someone* – is feeding off the talent in London's music scene.

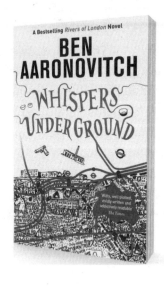

#3 WHISPERS UNDER GROUND:

An American art student has been killed at the Baker Street Underground station. It isn't long before Peter's investigation leads him into the tunnels beneath the city, only for him to discover far more than he bargained for about London's historic Tube network.

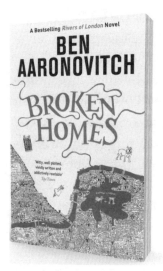

#4 BROKEN HOMES:

There's a killer on the loose, and Peter suspects they're linked to the criminal he has come to call the Faceless Man. But things get stranger when he is called to investigate something odd at a housing estate in Elephant and Castle, something which might bring Peter's world crashing down around him . . .

'A charming, witty and exciting romp through a magical world' *The Independent*

#5 FOXGLOVE SUMMER:

Two eleven-year-old girls have gone missing in rural Herefordshire. When it becomes clear this is no ordinary crime, Peter Grant is called to investigate. Whether he wants to leave the capital or not.

#6 THE HANGING TREE:

A group of teenagers break into a luxury apartment, and Peter is called in when one dies of an overdose. Ordinary policing, he believes. Except the death is far more magical than first meets the eye, and he is dragged into a world he would rather have stayed well shot of.

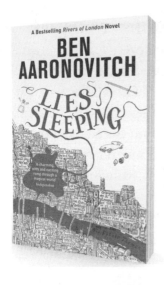

#7 LIES SLEEPING

The Faceless Man has been unmasked, and is on the run. But even as Peter bears down on his foe, he uncovers clues that, far from being finished, they are executing the final stages of a long-term plan.

#8 FALSE VALUE

Leaving his old police life behind, Peter takes a job with Terrence Skinner's new London start up, the Serious Cybernetics Corporation, and is drawn into the orbit of Old Street's famous 'silicon roundabout'. Compared to his last job, Peter thinks it should be a doddle. But magic is not finished with the Met's first trainee wizard in fifty years . . .

#9 AMONGST OUR WEAPONS

The London Silver Vaults is not a place where you can murder someone and vanish without a trace. The disappearing act and memory loss amongst the witnesses make this a case for Peter Grant. But Peter is about to encounter something – and somebody – that nobody ever expects . . .

'A darkly comic read with characters you can't help but like' *The Sunday Express*

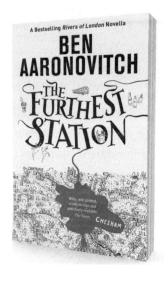

NOVELLA #1
THE FURTHEST STATION

There's something going bump on the Metropolitan line, and despite calling the police themselves, the traumatised commuters quickly forget their strange encounter. Cue Peter Grant's arrival, who is all geared up for a ghost hunt, even if it's as far from London as the Tube will go.

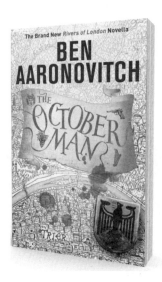

NOVELLA #2
THE OCTOBER MAN

Trier is a quiet German city. So when a corpse is found, impossibly covered in fungal rot, the local police know they are out of their depth. Enter Investigator Tobias Winter, who intends to solve things with the minimum of fuss and paperwork. Trier itself, though, might have other plans . . .

'Wise, witty and utterly absorbing' *Daily Mail*

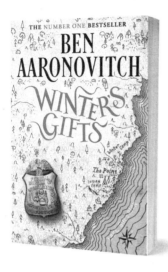

NOVELLA #3
WINTER'S GIFTS:
When ex-FBI Agent Patrick Henderson calls in an 'X-Ray Sierra India' incident, Special Agent Kimberley Reynolds doesn't understand. Arriving in snowy Wisconsin, she finds no sign of Henderson. Neighbours report unsettling sightings and the snow keeps rising – soon cutting off the town, with no way in or out . . .

DISCOVER LONDON'S DARKEST SECRETS...

FROM BEST-SELLING WRITER **BEN AARONOVITCH**
AND *DOCTOR WHO* CONTRIBUTORS **ANDREW CARTMEL** & **LEE SULLIVAN**

ACTION AT A DISTANCE
On Sale Now
£13.99
ISBN: 9781785865466

WATER WEED
On Sale Now
£13.99
ISBN: 9781785865459

CRY FOX
On Sale Now
£13.99
ISBN: 9781785861727

DETECTIVE STORIES
On Sale Now
£13.99
ISBN: 9781785861710

BLACK MOULD
On Sale Now
£13.99
ISBN: 9781785855108

NIGHT WITCH
On Sale Now
£13.99
ISBN: 9781785852930

BODY WORK
On Sale Now
£10.99
ISBN: 9781782761877

AVAILABLE IN PRINT AND DIGITALLY AT
TITAN-COMICS.COM

Rivers of London © Ben Aaronovitch 2018.

Help us make the next generation of readers

We – both author and publisher – hope you enjoyed this book.
We believe that you can become a reader at any time in your life,
but we'd love your help to give the next generation a head start.

Did you know that 9% of children don't have a book of their
own in their home, rising to 13% in disadvantaged families*?
We'd like to try to change that by asking you to consider the role
you could play in helping to build readers of the future.

We'd love you to think of sharing, borrowing, reading, buying or talking
about a book with a child in your life and spreading the love of reading.
We want to make sure the next generation continue to have access
to books, wherever they come from.

And if you would like to consider donating to charities that help
fund literacy projects, find out more at www.literacytrust.org.uk
and www.booktrust.org.uk.

Thank you.

hachette
CHILDREN'S GROUP

*As reported by the National Literacy Trust